I0649239

Roberts Brothers

A Newport aquarelle

Roberts Brothers

A Newport aquarelle

ISBN/EAN: 9783743304956

Manufactured in Europe, USA, Canada, Australia, Japa

Cover: Foto ©Andreas Hilbeck / pixelio.de

Manufactured and distributed by brebook publishing software
(www.brebook.com)

Roberts Brothers

A Newport aquarelle

THE CASINO, NEWPORT.

BOSTON:
ROBERTS BROTHERS.
1883.

Cambridge:
PRINTED BY JOHN WILSON AND SON,
UNIVERSITY PRESS.

could pick you out a New York girl from a
crowd of specimen women from every town
in England and America. They have a way
of holding their elbows, and a certain half-
arrogant, half-flirtatious, entirely fetching
poise of the head, that beats all the other
women in creation."

" I being a New Yorker, thank you for the
compliment. Do you think Gladys Carleton
a beauty ? "

" Perhaps I should if *you* were not here ; I
can hardly tell. My eyes are rather dazzled.
If Miss Carleton is your friend, won't you
present me to her ? "

The lady addressed seemed not altogether
pleased at this request, but she answered, —

" Oh yes ; I will stop her when she passes
back this way. I cannot leave my seat, or I
shall never get another."

The speakers were seated in the long cres-
cent-shaped corridor of the Newport Casino.
The hands of the quaint golden clock on the
tower of the outer courtyard pointed to the

A NEWPORT AQUARELLE

CHAPTER I.

"WHO is that tall girl with Mrs. Fallow-Deer?"

"You have been in Newport twenty-four hours and don't know? Why, that is Gladys Carleton. You 've heard of her, of course?"

"Can't say I have. A New York belle, I suppose, from her get-up?"

"Yes; her ambition is to be taken for an English girl, though, of course, you detected the spurious imitation of your countrywomen. At what point does the Anglo veneer fail to cover the American girl?"

"I should n't say she was veneered at all, but she 's a typical New Yorker. I can't tell you exactly where the difference lies, but I

hour of twelve. It was mid-day, and all the
fashionable world of Newport was gathered
within the aristocratic enclosure just named.
Some of the more energetic people were playing lawn tennis in the fine grounds of the
inner courtyard, which separates the semi-
circle of the open corridor from the theatre
and racket court. Others were lunching
luxuriously in the well-appointed restaurant,
and a few of the more serious-minded butterflies were sitting in the comfortable reading-
room, where ladies, as well as gentlemen, are
admitted to read the news, and write their
impressions of the place to their less fortunate friends and relatives, broiling in town or
rusticating in Maine. But the great crowd
of people were assembled in the open corridor, listening to the music of the band, which
at that moment was playing the exhilarat-
ing strains of the " Merry War." Seated on
either side was a double row of people, who
laughed and chatted with each other, criticis-
ing the less fortunate late-comers who had

found no seats, these last having no other
resource than to walk up and down between
the two rows of well-dressed men and women. The most popular of the ladies held
little courts of their own at different points
of the corridor, and were surrounded by
circles of men, of whom they spoke to their
husbands as friends, to their lady acquaint-
ances as beaux.

The lady who had promised to stop. Miss
Carleton as she passed by, had succeeded in
securing for herself a seat close to the steps
which led down from the corridor to the tennis courts, — a veritable coigne of vantage,
from whence every eligible man who passed
up or down the steps could be arrested by a
smile or a word. She had hurried her toilet
in order to be early on the ground and make
sure of the coveted spot. It was not to be
wondered at that she was not in haste to
surrender it, in order to oblige Mr. Cuthbert
Larkington by an introduction to Gladys
Carleton. She did not intend to surrender

either her seat or her cavalier, for Larkington was certainly the most stylish-looking man in the whole Casino, and was, besides, sure to become the lion of the season. He had arrived in Newport only the day before, bringing a letter to Mrs. Fallow-Deer. He had been told that the only thing necessary to open all doors in that exclusive society to an Englishman was the patronage of this distinguished lady. Mrs. Fallow-Deer had a right to the high position she held in Newport society. She was by birth a Van Schuylkill, of New York, and belonged to one of the old Dutch families, who had always stood well in Manhattan, since the days when their ancestor, Peter Van Schuylkill, came out among the earliest settlers. In her youth Miss Van Schuylkill had accompanied her father to England, whither he had been sent as American Minister, and while there she had been sought in marriage by Mr. Fallow-Deer, an English gentleman, of large fortune. After thirty years of wedded

life in the mother country, Mrs. Fallow-Deer
had returned to the home of her youth, a
widow, and a very rich woman. She had
soon made her house in New York one of
the most attractive in the city. A social
leader she was born to be, always had been,
and was likely to die in harness. She had
certain eccentricities, but was essentially conventional in thought and conversation; she
had talked so much society talk that it was
impossible for her to doff her worldly manner and her social vernacular, which she
carried into her most intimate domestic
life. From her long residence in England,
she had come to be considered by the men
and women of her set as a sort of oracle of
les convenances.

On arriving, Mr. Larkington had called at
Mrs. Fallow-Deer's to deposit his card, his
letter, and a bunch of flowers, which Fadden
the florist assured him was the finest bouquet
he had made up that season. The result of
his attention had been an invitation to din-

ner that very evening, which he had accepted with dignified effusion. He had taken his *Anglophilic* hostess down to dinner, and listened with respect and attention to her six-month-stale stories of the sayings and doings of H. R. H. the Prince of Wales, and the worshipful members of his especial set. Larkington had found a good deal of amusement during the dinner in his right-hand neighbor. She was a pretty woman of the Venus de Médicis type, which is by no means uncommon among American women.

Mrs. Craig was not beautiful, though he had told her before the dessert that she was; but she was the perfection of prettiness. Small, without being undersized, with charming curves of face and figure, a well-shaped face and head, blond hair, deep-gray eyes, and a mouth which, though well cut, was too narrow and bloodless to betoken a generous or passionate nature. She had received the Englishman's attentions with cordiality and friendliness, and had promised, as he escorted

her to her carriage, to meet him at the Casino
the next morning at twelve o'clock.

Mrs. Craig had found Larkington awaiting her at the entrance of the Casino, and,
after one anxious glance, had become reas-
sured, and laughed at her own fears lest he
should not be "presentable by daylight."

"In the evening," Mrs. Craig had argued
to herself, "any man can look swell; but it
is the morning dress which really shows
his social status and the club to which he
belongs."

Mrs. Craig had not exaggerated the effect
which her entrance with the distinguished-
looking "new arrival" would make on the
crowd of people at the Casino, already tired
of each other's faces, though the season was
but three weeks old. The women all stopped
talking as she passed, and the men looked
curiously at "the new Englishman Mrs.
Craig had in tow." If the lady's manner
had on the previous evening been cordial
to Mr. Larkington, it might now have been

called familiar; for, conscious that the eyes of all her friends and enemies were centred upon her, she assumed that air of condescending possession which women of her nature show to the men with whom their names are more or less connected. During the first half-hour things had gone very well, and she had remained in undisturbed possession of the new man, who was — greater triumph — an Englishman. She had introduced him to her husband, who came "clumbering" along, to use one of her coinages of language, to Mr. Belhomme, the Master of the Hounds, to the respected President of the Casino, and to the ruling spirit of the Redwood Club.

These gentlemen had all received Larkington with cordiality and consideration, and Mrs. Craig had the ineffable joy of stealing Mrs. Fallow-Deer's thunder, and playing patroness to the good-looking foreigner. But her triumph was short-lived; and when Mrs. Fallow-Deer appeared upon the scene, bearing down with full sail to a spot where chairs were quickly placed for her and her companion, Gladys Carleton, the eyes of the prize roamed anxiously in their direction.

Mrs. Craig was on her mettle: the equivocal expression with which she looked full into the eyes of Larkington was one which she rarely allowed herself to use in society; and the laughter which babbled from her lips was silver-sweet in tone, but when she spoke her voice was sharpened by anxiety.

Mrs. Fallow-Deer, having seated her ample person, and spread out her gorgeous raiment, soon espied the group of which Mrs. Craig was the centre, and, having attracted Larkington's attention, gave him a superb, rocking-horse bow, full of consideration and sweetness. The true state of affairs at once became evident to her, and, turning to the bearer of her fan, a young aspirant to fashion, she said, " Won't you kindly ask Mrs. Craig if she can tell me the hour of the rendezvous for the picnic to-morrow? "

The move was a successful one. Mrs.
Craig, turning to speak to the young myr-
midon, Larkington was left untrammelled
by her wooing glance, and with a hurried
" Excuse me for one moment," he crossed
the corridor and entered the enemy's lines.

" So glad to see you here, Mr. Larkington ;
is it not a pretty scene ? But of course, after
Cowes, it seems very small to you. Still, I
think it is not quite unlike the grounds of
the Royal Yacht Squadron; how does it
strike you ? "

" I think that the Club garden never had
such a compliment before, Mrs. Fallow-Deer ;
we have nothing in England that compares
with Newport. It is really a sort of modern
Pompeii, where all the rich Americans come
to play at taking a rest."

" It is very good-natured of you to say such
nice things, I am sure. I want to present
you to Miss Carleton, who is my guest.
Gladys, let me present the Hon. Mr. Cuthbert Larkington, of Oxfordshire."

The two young people bowed, — the man
lifting his hat and making a deep obeisance,
the girl moving her graceful head perhaps a
quarter of an inch, and looking with an air
of composed observance into the face of the
dark, striking-looking stranger. Whether he
chose to admit it to Mrs. Craig or not, Larkington was much impressed with the beauty
of Gladys Carleton. He instinctively compared her to the Arab mare which had borne
him many miles over the deserts of Syria,
and which he had cared for rather more than
for any other living creature.

She was tall, straight as an arrow, and
slender, long-limbed, with a small, round
waist, wide shoulders, and full, classic bust,
carefully displayed by the close-fitting dress
of dark-blue foulard, fastened at the throat
with a pair of deep sapphire buttons. Her
head was magnificently set on her shoulders,
and its poise was, to quote the phrase Larkington had used, "half arrogant and wholly
fetching." The head itself was small, and,

if not intellectual, intelligent in shape. Her fine black hair was brushed simply back from her temples, — she could afford to show her brow. Her eyes were dark and full of fire; the thick line of the eyebrows not classic, but effective. The straight, sensitive nose, with its red nostrils, showed what her friends called her "high spirit;" her maid vulgarly referred to it as a mark of her "ugly temper." Her mouth was full and red, curved and dainty, — a beauty rarely found among the women of her race. Her tiny roseleaf ears had never been desecrated by the needle of the jeweller, and the faultless teeth showed no trace of a dentist's care. A singularly striking-looking woman, whose age *might* be anywhere from eighteen to twenty-eight, and was exactly a quarter of a century.

When Larkington looked at the smooth fleckless skin, he thought that she could not have passed her teens. Her assured and self-reliant bearing contradicted this supposition, and betokened much experience of the world.

"I was so sorry to miss you at dinner last evening, — I was dining at Mrs. Belhomme's. Mrs. Fallow-Deer told me how you amused them all, and has promised to ask you again very soon for my special benefit. Do you think you will like Newport?"

"I know I shall; in fact, I do. I am almost at home here already."

"You will feel yourself quite at home this afternoon, I fancy, for it is the first hunt of the season. Of course you are going?"

"If you are, Miss Carleton, I am, of course. But what sort of a hunt is it, — a butterfly hunt? Considering the season, I suppose the game must have golden wings."

"Butterflies? Oh no! we are not cannibals at Newport, and do not kill our kind. The hunt is a real hunt as far as the prey is concerned. The only sham part of it is the scent, which is that of a red herring dragged across the fields by a huntsman on the morning of the meet."

" So the route is all laid out? and how does the fox — it is a fox? — well, how does he understand that he must follow the scent of the herring? Does your system of compulsory education extend to the members of the animal kingdom ? "

" Do not be satirical, Mr. Larkington. Of course, the whole thing sounds very absurd to you; but as we have no foxes in this neighborhood, we import the poor little beasts. The fox is conveyed in a leathern bag to a certain spot agreed upon, and when we have all begun to think that herring scent is a poor sort of game, out springs Mr. Reynard a field beyond, and we all take heart, — hounds, horses, and riders, — and plunge after him with renewed ardor. If the fox part of it is a sham, I can say more for the riding. Newport is the roughest country I have ever hunted in. Have you your horse with you ? "

" Yes, I bought a couple of hunters in New York; they arrived yesterday, and I

shall most certainly join the hunt this afternoon.   Do the men wear the pink ? "

" Yes ; most of them.   It makes the spectacle so much gayer, and the pink coats set
off the dark habits very prettily.   They are
not always becoming, but then one ought to
be willing to sacrifice one's self to the general picturesqueness of the landscape."

Catching the last part of this sentence,
Mrs. Fallow-Deer, who had been occupied in
scanning with half-closed eyes the groups
of people scattered about the lawn, broke
into the conversation.

" Yes, it is a picturesque scene, is it not ?
But I want to present you, Mr. Larkington,
to one of its most picturesque objects, Mrs.
Belhomme.   I am going to take you to a
reception at her house this evening.   I 'll be
back again, Gladys ; keep my seat for me."

And the great woman sailed away on the
arm of her new protégé.   Poor little Mrs.
Craig grew pale as the couple swept past
her.   Her only cavalier for the moment hap-

pened to be Mr. Craig, her devoted and long-suffering husband; and this fact added gall to the wormwood of her defeat. She was somewhat soothed, however, by the approach of Count Clawski, a foreign diplomate with a high official position. This gentleman, after the formalities of the morning greeting, inquired of Mrs. Craig the name and station of the tall Englishman, who was the subject of general conversation that morning. Mrs. Craig assured him that she was in no way responsible for the gentleman, whom she had met at dinner the evening before at Mrs. Fallow-Deer's, and whom she had *accidentally* encountered at the entrance of the Casino. Count Clawski had lived in England, and knew of an aristocratic family of the name of Larkington.

Mrs. Craig now being quite ready to leave the Casino, the Count escorted her to her carriage, and made his most respectful obeisance to the pretty woman, who nodded a flirtatious farewell, and, saying to her footman,

" Go to the Redwood Library," was rolled
away in her luxurious Victoria to that vener-
able and stately edifice.

Entering the quaint old library, Mrs. Craig
asked the custodian for a book, which was
quickly brought her, and, seating herself at
a table, the pretty woman soon became absorbed in the perusal of that volume which
in importance ranks with the book of Common Prayer in all English households. Does
not the British Peerage contain between its
covers the Alpha and Omega of every true
Briton's social creed, which should profess a
belief in the Queen and Empress of all the
important parts of the earth ; a belief in the
House of Lords, the aristocracy and all their
friends; a faith and reverence for all the
decrees of H. R. H. the Prince of Wales, and
his set ?

CHAPTER II.

IT was a perfect Newport afternoon. The sun, which had shone brightly all the morning, had drawn a veil of soft gray clouds before his face, and a cool west wind blew refreshingly over the road, whose dust had been laid by a shower during the night.

The West Road, which leads from the town of Newport out into the quiet country, was dotted here and there with groups of riders, and with carriages of all degrees, from trotting-wagons to four-in-hand coaches.

All the vehicles were wending their way to Southwick's Grove, the spot appointed for that afternoon's meet.

It was early as yet, only half-past four o'clock, and the road was not crowded by the hurrying late-comers.

There were a few among the riders and
drivers who could appreciate the views which
are to be had from different points on the
road.

At the bend which marks the boundary
between the townships of Newport and Mid-
dletown, two riders had drawn rein, and
were looking out over the stretches of warm-
hued meadow-land which lie between the
high-road and the waters of the bay.

The bold outline of the hill on the right,
and the group of dark green trees on the left
of the riders, made a frame for the great life-
picture of sea, sky, and meadow, at which
they looked half understandingly.

The high rocky island of Conanicut, with
the ruined fort of the Dumplings on its
summit, lay before them, outlined against
pearly gray clouds, the sea of a deeper gray
washing softly about its base. A swift-
winged boat, with a flock of white sea-gulls
wheeling about its bow, came skimming
across the picture, and added the charm of
motion to the scene.

A little puff of smoke floated low down beneath the clouds, and as they looked the white prow of a steamer parted the gray waves, and swiftly crossed the line of their vision. A sudden scream of a steam whistle fell upon the quiet air, and the spell was broken, the charm of the picture was gone.

Slowly, regretfully, the eyes of the young woman in the trig blue habit turned from the far-off peaceful scene, broken by the prosaic sight and sound of the steamer, and, following the long lines of brown and green meadow-land, dwelt a moment on the group of men and boys at work near by, and then looked into the face of her companion.

"Is it not beautiful, Cid? and to think that I have ridden past this spot twenty times this summer, and never noticed the view! You are never too busy to miss one glimpse of the beauty which you say the world is full of, and *I* have to be told that what I see is lovely before my dulness can understand it. All the lovely things I have seen in my life, you have shown me."

The eyes of the speaker, Gladys Carleton, were so soft at that moment that the man by her side wondered if the hard, bold look, which was their dominant expression, was not one acquired by habit and external influences, and this wistful, half-tender expression their natural one. He had often before asked himself this question, and had always answered it sadly in the negative. And yet the query came again to his mind on that fair summer afternoon, and was not to be dismissed so easily as it had been.

Charles Farwell, called by Gladys Carleton "Cid," was a handsome man of thirty, with certain traits which distinguished him from the hundred or two young New Yorkers who were at that time infesting Newport.

He was of the pure Saxon type sometimes found among our people, with golden hair and beard, fair skin, and eyes of that intense blue which is only seen with people of vigorous temperament. His features were almost too delicate for a man, but his six

feet of height and broad shoulders, his strong
well-modelled arms and legs, saved him from
the charge of a too feminine beauty.

His expression was open and simple, and
his bearing frank and natural. There was
a tendency to dreaminess in the face, concerning whose beauty he honestly neither
thought nor cared. His cousin Gladys had
told him that a beautiful woman who was
not vain was a *rara avis* indeed, but that a
handsome man without vanity was a creature too unnatural, too absolutely *sui generis*,
to be popular among men or women.

Charles Farwell and Gladys Carleton were
of a convenient kinship, being second cousins. A second cousin may always be that
dimly anticipated " Fate " which haunts the
minds of all young people, and there is an
easy familiarity in the relation, which may
remain but a pleasant feature in their lives,
and yet can easily deepen into a controlling
association.

These two young people had lived as

children on opposite sides of the then fashionable quarter of Gramercy Park, and had
played together in the dusty city garden
through the long days when from Sunday
to Sunday seemed half a lifetime.   They
had fallen in love of course, and when
Gladys was seventeen and Farwell twenty-
two, there had been an " understanding "
between them.   This was one of those
" understandings " into which American girls
are apt to enter, sometimes with more than
one man at a time, in which the maiden
is left quite free, and the man is bound
unconditionally.

Gladys did not know her own mind, —
how could she, not having seen anything
of the world?   She *thought* she loved her
cousin, and was sure she cared more for
him than for any other man, — but she could
not promise.

Well, he would wait (they always do);
and after waiting for three years, during
which time he had the doubtful happiness

of corresponding with his lovely cousin, of
sending her flowers, and of seeing her dance
at balls with other men, his roses held
against her cheek and their shoulders, —
after all this he still held only the position
of her acknowledged admirer, among many
others.

She would drive with him in the park,
if she were not engaged to drive with any
one else; when she had an off evening, she
telegraphed for him to take herself and her
sister to the play.

In the early summer he was privileged
to spend a long month with her at the old
homestead in Rhode Island, where an old
relative, the Rev. Abel Carleton, lived.

In this quiet spot Gladys recruited her
strength for the Newport season.

Farwell was looked upon in the family as
the hopeless adorer of his cousin. Neither
her worldly mother nor her sisters doubted for
a moment that Gladys would make a great
match; but meanwhile Cousin Charlie was a

dear good fellow, generous with his three thousand a year, honorable, and so chivalrous that Gladys had given him the nickname of Cid in the days in which he had read to her the wonderful stories of the prowess of the fabled hero. Cid he had always been called by the Carletons, who all really loved him, when they had time to think about it, and he stood to them somewhat in the relation of the " property man " in the company of a theatre, the person to be called on at all times, for all necessities.

At first Farwell had been sure of Gladys; after she had seen something of society and had " had her fling," she would give it all up, marry him, and settle down somewhere out of town, where they could live very comfortably on their joint income (that of Gladys sufficed for her wardrobe), and lead the happy, quiet domestic life for which he fancied they were both suited.

But as time wore on, and Gladys grew colder and harder, and more thoroughly a

woman of the world, hope grew faint, and
finally on her twentieth birthday they had
taken a long walk together, and had talked
the matter out. The understanding was
now altered, and Farwell realized that Gladys
was in earnest when she told him that "for
two such beggars, with nothing a year, to
speak about marriage would be sheer lunacy."

He had taken the disappointment very
hard, and was thankful when the Carletons
soon after decided to make a trip to Europe.
It was easier to forget it all with her far
away from him.

Gladys had been "a great success" in
England, in Paris, in Rome, — wherever she
went. She had been twice engaged, and had
just missed becoming "my lady" by the in-
triguings of a sister of the young Earl who
had fallen in love with her. The other
lover whom she had accepted and finally
discarded was a German banker of enormous wealth and high standing. Neverthe-
less, when the time appointed for the mar-

riage drew near, Gladys had been seized with a horror of her plighted lover, and taking her maid with her had fled from Berlin to London, leaving her mother to settle the difficulty, while she amused the London friend to whose house she had been welcomed on her arrival, with mimicry of ponderous Herr Goldzchink's ponderous wooings.

The story of her escapade was soon known, and she became the belle of the London season, dined at Marlboro' House, and afterwards received more invitations than would have sufficed three American belles.

Six months before the opening of our story, Mrs. Carleton, somewhat discouraged, be it said, by her want of success in the matrimonial market, had found it necessary to return to America and attend to some urgent business matters.

Gladys had become in these six months quite at home again in the country which she had not seen in as many years, and after a winter in New York had passed a month at the old homestead as in other days. Having accepted Mrs. Fallow-Deer's invitation to pass the month of August with her at Newport, she was enjoying for the first time in several years the brilliant entertainments of our summer city. She found that things had changed much during her absence, and felt, as she had never done before, the great difficulty which people with moderate means find in maintaining their place in a society which has become vulgarized by the vast quantities of wealth brought into it by uncultivated people.

The tone of the society seemed also to have become in a certain sense Europeanized, and she did not find the great contrast she had expected; Newport manners and customs, unlike those of the Medes and Persians, having changed considerably.

" I find people here much broader than I remember them to have been," Gladys had said to her cousin.

"Yes," Cid had rather grimly replied; "you will find people here just as broad as you will allow them to be," — for which remark he had been promptly and properly snubbed.

As the two young people gave their horses the rein, a carriage rolled by them, in which were seated Mrs. Craig and Mrs. Fallow-Deer; the latter called out to Gladys, —

"You are late, dear! You must trot along very fast, or they will be off without you."

An excellent horsewoman was Gladys Carleton, and she never appeared to more advantage than when in the saddle. At Mrs. Fallow-Deer's warning, she touched her tall sorrel lightly with her crop, and the two young people rode off at a sharp pace. Arriving at the rendezvous, they found a large group of riders, twenty or thirty men, and half as many women, all well mounted and well got up.

Some of the gentlemen wore pink coats, others were in plain riding-dress. The huntsmen were busy with the hounds, a fine pack imported from Buckinghamshire, and the hunters were talking and laughing together, walking their horses about, or tightening their girths for the long run.

In the large open space of the grove hundreds of carriages, filled with spectators, were assembled, and more were arriving every moment. The horns of the coaches sounded merrily in the distance, and presently a drag, driven by a wounded polo-player, his crutches conspicuously displayed beside him, rolled into the grove.

On this coach the quick eyes of Gladys Carleton espied her English acquaintance of the morning, the Hon. Cuthbert Larkington.

Mr. Larkington's horse, having been led out by a groom, was awaiting him. He sprang into the saddle and joined the group of riders, making his way to the side of Gladys, by whom he was half-graciously received.

She never was quite gracious to any one.
An introduction to Farwell followed, and as
the two gentlemen bowed, the horns of the
huntsmen warned them that the run was
about to begin.

Off went the hounds across the road,
scrambling over the loose stone-wall which
divided it from the field.

They ran sniffing and crying at the herring scent, as if they knew all about the im-
posture practised on them, and resented it.

After them followed the riders, men and
women. The wall was not a very high one,
and the horses leaped lightly over it, no one
coming to grief.

The carriages by this time were all tearing
down the high-road, which was also lined
with a number of riders, who followed the
hunt from this safe vantage-ground, endan-
gering nothing but their eyesight, which the
cloud of dust threatened, and enjoying the
hunt quite as much as its followers, — so
they affirmed.

Gladys was among the foremost riders, and Farwell and Larkington pressed their horses to keep at her side.

Away they galloped across stubble-fields and open meadows, taking a five-barred gate here, and a water jump there, as they came. No side roads or opened gates for Gladys; she loved the excitement of the run as much as did her sorrel, Nimbus.

He was a splendid beast, strong, powerfully built, and in fine condition.

Before they had ridden three miles it became apparent to both of the cavaliers that Gladys had the best mount, and it was with difficulty that the two men kept at her side.

She spoke to Larkington occasionally, but oftener to her horse, which she encouraged by calling his name constantly. At last, after a run of about seven miles, during which several ugly croppers were taken by some of the riders and horses, a little puppy fox was seen to issue from the leathern bag in which he had been confined, a field ahead of the hunting party.

The hounds leaped forward at a quicker pace, crying at the sight of their prey, and the men and women spurred their horses on for the last field.

Excited exclamations escaped from the men as they lashed their tired steeds, and a cry of "Go on, Nimbus!" fell on Farwell's ear. It had come from the lips of Gladys; and as he looked at her, he wondered where the tender expression could have vanished which had stirred his heart an hour ago.

She was flushed, and her eyes sparkled with excitement. She struck her horse and urged him over the last wall as a jockey might have done, and with the cry which he had heard, and which had no sound of her natural voice in it, she swept across the field even with the huntsmen, and leading the whole cavalcade.

And the fox? well, he was only a stupid little creature after all, and, quite dazed by the sudden light, by the cries of the hounds, and the approach of all these men, women, and horses, he did nothing but jump up on the stone wall and look wonderingly at the superior animals who had come so far to find him.

When the pack were close upon him he realized what it all meant, — that it was to take his miserable little life that all these great creatures — brave men and delicate women, hounds and horses — had come out on this bright summer afternoon.

He realized it, but too late even to try for an escape. He looked about him over a strange open country with fields on either side, and, seeing how hopeless it was, stood quite still, looking at the animals, guided by their king, man, who were now close upon him.

One great cry he gave as he felt the teeth of the foremost hound fasten on his throat, and then all was over, and in a space of time something less than sixty

seconds, the Master of the Hunt approached
Miss Carleton with the brush of the fox,
which she hung at the pommel of her
saddle.

As they all rode home together through
the quiet country lanes, little children ran
to the doors of the farm-houses and looked
admiringly at the cavalcade.

The feathered creatures, just preparing to
go to rest in the arms of the great trees,
flapped their wings angrily at the dust and
disturbance created on the highway, which
after six o'clock was deserted save on the
days of the hunt.

An apple orchard on the right side of
the road lay between the riders and the
setting sun.

The light falling in low, slanting rays
between the shadows of the wonderful old
gnarled trees, gray and twisted, gave a color
to the grass which is found nowhere in
the world save in the island of Rhode
Island, — a color as of a million emeralds

softened and deepened by the yellow light of the setting sun.

"If I were obliged to say what was the most beautiful thing in all Newport, I should say the turf of this orchard, in the afternoon."

Gladys was the speaker.

"And you say that you never see anything that is beautiful," Farwell remarked.

"I should n't have seen it if I had not been with you, Cid."

As they rode down Bellevue Avenue to Mrs. Fallow-Deer's house, which was situated on the cliffs, Larkington made himself very agreeable to Farwell, who received the advances of the Englishman cordially.

The two gentlemen then took leave of Miss Carleton, Farwell lifting her from her horse in a matter-of-course manner.

At the moment in which her palm lay upon his shoulder, and his hands spanned her slender waist, she gave a little tired sigh, almost like a child's. She smiled with her eyes as well as her lips in that brief instant when her face was so near to his, and though she gave her hand to Larkington at parting, and only nodded *him* a good-night, Cid rode away with his heart beating fast, his whole being quickened by the influence of that tired sigh, that deep smile.

Farwell felt so much at peace with the world in general, and in especial with the man who had *not* lifted Gladys from her horse, that in a moment of expansiveness he asked Larkington to dine with him at the restaurant of the Casino.

The invitation was accepted, and the two men passed the evening together, playing a game of billiards after dinner.

Farwell was rightly counted by the men of his club as an excellent player, but he found that in Larkington he had met more than his match. Though Larkington had taken twice as much wine as he had at dinner, his strokes seemed as steady as those of a professional billiard-player.

The stranger's game was so remarkable that quite a group of men collected round the table to watch it. After a few games in which he was rather badly beaten, Farwell remembered an engagement, and excusing himself left his new friend the centre of an admiring group, and walked off to his lodgings over the baker's shop in John Street.

They were comfortable rooms enough, the little bedroom and parlor which he had hired for the months of August and September, and he threw himself into the black horsehair rocking-chair, which his landlady had lent him from her own sitting-room, and lighting his pipe divested himself of his coat and boots, — a thing which every true-born American does immediately on entering the privacy of his own apartment.

Something besides the smile of Gladys had occurred to please Charles Farwell. Loving her as he had all his life, and understanding her as thoroughly as he did, her kindness and her unkindness usually depressed him equally, when the charm of her presence was removed.

If she was, as she had been that day, almost tender to him, the old conviction, always latent in his mind, that she really loved him, would assert itself, and the feeling that if he chose to exert his will, he could induce her to marry him, would grow into a certainty.

But with this certainty came also the remembrance of the great, insuperable objection to such a step, — that of his limited income, which to her meant poverty.

He knew that to her luxurious nature any enforced economy would be irksome, perhaps intolerable, and feared lest it might imbitter her character, whose selfish impulses he knew so well.

He would not now, with his knowledge of the world and its men and women, beg her to renounce it all, for love and for him.

That he himself was generous to a fault, giving away his money whenever he had any to give, and working year in and year out in a broker's office in Wall Street in order that his sisters might have his share of the income from his father's estate, made him none the less aware of the selfish side of Gladys's nature.

He could make her marry him, — of that he was sure now, — but could he make her happy? As if to answer the self-asked question he drew from his pocket a crumpled bit of paper, and read for the third time a despatch which he had that afternoon received, and which ran as follows : —

LEADVILLE, Aug. 19, 1882.

To CHARLES FARWELL,
    Redwood Reading Room,
      Newport, R. I.

New lead discovered ; assay yields 20 per cent of silver. Come at once.

CARTWRIGHT.

CHAPTER III.

On the morning following the fox-hunt, Mr. Larkington, inquiring at the post-office for letters, was somewhat surprised at the large bundle of notes which the clerk put into his hand.

He glanced hurriedly over the addresses: there was one foreign letter, with an English postmark, directed in a pointed feminine hand.

This letter he impatiently tore open, unfolding it without glancing at the writing, and looked between the closely written pages of the sheet.

Here he found a narrow slip of paper, which the lady clerk observed afterwards to the postmaster "was a check, as any one could see."

Whether this lady was right in her hypothesis or not, the perusal of the narrow bit of paper seemed to have an agreeable effect upon Mr. Larkington. His face, which until then had been rather moody, cleared, and, folding the paper, he placed it carefully in his pocket-book, thrust the unread letter which had been so carefully written, into his pocket, and proceeded to open leisurely the other notes.

All of these bore the local postmark.

The first one was marked by an elaborate crest, in blue and gold, and read as follows: "Mrs. Craig requests the pleasure of Mr. Larkington's company at dinner on Monday evening next, at half-past seven."

Another informed him that "Mrs. Fallow-Deer hopes that Mr. Larkington will drive with her on Saturday afternoon."

A third read: "Mr. Belhomme will be very glad to lend Mr. Larkington his coach and horses on Friday and Saturday of this week, during his absence in New York."

There were half a dozen other invitations
to balls and routs of various kinds, and, most
important of all to the mind of the Englishman, invitations for a month to the Redwood
and Casino Clubs.   To the first of these,
incorrectly called the " Reading Room,"
Larkington immediately repaired.

Here he was warmly greeted by the men
whose acquaintance he had made on the previous day and evening.   These gentlemen
introduced him to others.

Cuthbert Larkington had come to Newport, forty-eight hours before, a stranger, with
no further claim on society than that implied
by a single letter of introduction.

This letter, which was addressed to Mrs.
Fallow-Deer, had been given him by a
steamer acquaintance, to whom he had lent
twenty-five pounds.   He now felt that he
had gained a footing from which he could
climb to the heights of success and popu-
larity.

As he was leaving the Club, Larkington

met Count Clawski, and the two walked down
Bellevue Avenue together.

A carriage, drawn by a pair of magnificent
bay horses, rattled past them, the harnesses
jingling with enough chains to secure all the
prisoners in Newport jail.

Two ladies bowed from the back seat of
the carriage, and Larkington, recognizing the
face of the girl whose acquaintance he had
made the day before, made a deep obeisance;
Count Clawski, who seemed on good terms
with the ladies, waved his hat with airy grace.

" You have the good fortune to know Miss
Carleton, the heiress? " asked the Count.

" Yes; I met her yesterday. Is she one of
the very rich people here? "

" Oh yes; her fortune is counted in millions, — half a dozen, I believe, and it is all
in her own right. An interesting woman,
very. Her cousin is very pretty, is she
not? "

" I did not notice the cousin," answered
Larkington, absently. " Is she an orphan,

— Miss Carleton, — that she is so rich? From whom did she get all her money?"

"Oh, old Mr. Carleton was an enormously rich man, and she is his only child. She is an excellent woman of business, and manages her own affairs entirely. She has a mother; but Mrs. Carleton is not here this summer. She is an old lady, and finds Newport too exciting for her taste."

This is what was said on the sidewalk.

The lady in the carriage who was the subject of this conversation said to her companion, —

"Do you know who that man with Count Clawski is, Gladys?"

"Oh yes, Cousin Amelia; I can tell you all about him. His name is Larkington, — the Hon. Cuthbert Larkington. He is an Englishman, of high family. Mrs. Craig was telling us all about him this morning. She had been looking him up in the Peerage. He is the son of Lord Lucre, and is in the Army. I met him yesterday, and found him

quite agreeable. You ought to have him
presented, and ask him to dinner."

" I should be glad to know him, but I am
off for Lenox to-morrow. Would n't you
like to have Thomas come for you while I
am away? You can have the carriage every
afternoon, just as well as not. Mrs. Fallow-
Deer, with her numerous engagements, must
have constant use for hers."

Miss Amelia Carleton was the cousin of
Gladys, and Count Clawski had not exaggerated her fortune to Larkington.

She was a rather hard-favored iron-bound
virgin of some forty odd years, well preserved
and not the reverse of handsome in face or
figure. She had remained Miss Carleton
from choice, preferring the freedom of single
life and enjoying the power which her money
gave her. She could have married " anybody she pleased," as the phrase goes, but
she did not please, and said she did not care
to support any man for the pleasure of writing Mrs. before her name.

" There was, of course, some old romance," her friends all said, but who the hero of it was, even rumor whispered not.

It is quite possible that neither hero nor romance had ever entered her life.

She belonged to that type of women, not uncommon in New England, who do not feel the necessity of domestic relations for their happiness, and to whom men are rather antagonistic than attractive.

These women are often among the hardest workers in the social community, and are unremitting in their charitable labors. They are dubbed " strong-minded," — a title which they resent almost universally, and yet it is one they fully deserve.

It seems as though a wise provision of Providence had created a certain proportion of the women of the Eastern States with this independence of nature, to fit them for the life of moral and physical self-support imposed upon them by the disproportionately small number of men in these regions.

On reaching his hotel, Larkington walked slowly up the long stairs which led to the third floor, upon which his room was situated.

He seemed deeply absorbed in thought, and stood before the window, looking with unseeing eyes into the blue sky. Yet the tenor of his thoughts was of a nature more terrestrial than celestial, as the anxious expression of the eyes and lips betokened.

" Shall I, or shall I not, go in for the heiress ? " was the question he asked himself, as he paced slowly up and down the narrow coffin-like apartment, with its iron bedstead, chair, table, and wash-stand, for the use of which he would be obliged to pay five dollars a day, when he should settle his bill. When he should settle his bill! The thought reminded him of his unread letter, and seating himself at the table he soon became absorbed in the perusal of the finely crossed epistle.

After reading it through, he sat silent

for another space, staring out into the bright sunlight of the summer morning, and then quite suddenly drew toward him the pen and ink and paper, and rapidly indited the following note: —

DEAREST MUZ, — Thank you so much for the enclosure of one hundred pounds, and your kind letter, both this morning received. It is the last penny I'll ever ask you to send me, I swear that to you. I was pretty well cleaned out when it came, and never was gladder in my life to see your writing. Tell Sissy that I am going to make a dash for a fortune here. There's a pretty girl attached to it, to whom I can easily become attached. Failing this, I shall start for Mexico, and strike out for myself. I suppose Dad does n't suspect where I am ; don't let him know. Does n't he wonder who your feminine correspondent is ? Love to Sissy and your dear old self.

From your ever affectionate

CUTHBERT.

The letter was written in a small but bold hand. He directed the envelope in a large pointed lady-like chirography. It bore this superscription : —

> To Mrs. Martin Larkington,
> Care Larkington & Co.,
> No. 7 Washleather St.,
> Strand, London.

Now, if Mrs. Craig or Mrs. Fallow-Deer had happened to see this letter which their new acquaintance had just written to his mother, they would have been somewhat surprised at the business address which it bore. They would have looked for the following aristocratic superscription : —

> Lady Larkington Lucre,
> Larkington House,
> Larkington, Oxfordshire.

Having performed this filial duty, Larkington proceeded to look over the notes which he had so hurriedly read at the Post-Office. One there was which he had passed over, and on opening it he gave an exclamation of pleasure. The note was from Charles

Farwell, who offered Mr. Larkington the use of his two polo ponies during his absence, which would last for about two weeks, and telling him that a match was to take place that very afternoon, in which Farwell had arranged for Larkington to take his place.

If there was one pursuit which the Englishman cared for, more than any other in the world, it was certainly the game of polo.

Larkington was a tall athletic fellow, light of body and sinewy of limb. His arms and legs were long, and he had that grace of movement which comes only from a condition of perfect physical health and muscular development. Nimrod was his hero and his god. From hunting and athletic pursuits and sports he derived the greatest enjoyment of his life.

He was withal not lacking in other attainments which made him an agreeable man in a drawing-room, as well as a prominent one in the field. He had a gift for music

which, although uncultivated, was all the
more remarkable. He could play any air
that he had ever heard, with an *abandon*
and spirit which to unmusical people were
more captivating than the careful perform-
ance of a finished musician. He could talk
of English politics with a certain knowledge
of facts, but with an indifference to principles which proved that he was not guided
by them.

He was fairly well educated, had been at
a good public school, but had not passed
through a university.

He knew quite as much of Paris, Vienna,
and Rome, as of London, and seemed even
rather more at home in the society of these
European capitals than in that of London,
judging from his conversation concerning
them. He spoke — astonishing fact for
an Englishman ! — excellent French, good
German, and could make himself understood
in the other languages of Europe. His ideas
about art were absolutely without value.

Indeed, it should rather be said that he had none, being entirely wanting in artistic sense.

With all that belonged to nature he was in perfect sympathy, and his advice about the care of horses or cattle, and his comments on vegetables and fruit and the best manner of raising them, were well worth hearing.

Children liked him and came to him, as did dogs and all other uncivilized beings, but with women he was, strangely enough, not popular. He got on much better with men, and had had little to do with women. Of love in its higher form he knew nothing.

Five o'clock was the time appointed for polo, and at ten minutes past the hour, Larkington entered the grounds of the Westchester Polo Club, and rode down to the small pavilion tent, from the top of which floated a white flag. His faithful servant Stirrups, who was by turns his valet, groom, and companion, stood waiting him with

Charles Farwell's ponies. They were two sturdy little mustangs, with short cropped manes, and legs bandaged to the body for protection against the blows of the mallets.

One of his side told him that the match would not begin for a quarter of an hour, and Larkington took this opportunity of examining the ground which was soon to be turned into a battle-field. He had played polo in England and in Nice, but he affirmed to the men in the tent " that this ground beat all the others he had ever seen, hollow."

The large space of turf, which was outlined by strips of whitewash, marking the boundaries of the polo ground, was emerald green.

Outside of these lines was a wide driveway, with room enough for three or four carriages to stand abreast. A high fence surrounded the driveway, which was on this afternoon filled with carriages of every description.

The north side was reserved for the coaches,

of which a dozen were assembled, covered
with maids and matrons, in rainbow-hued
gowns and smart coaching-hats.

Equestrians were there, too, and a group of
people standing and sitting in the corner,
where stood a covered platform filled with
chairs.

The horses and their trappings were magnificent, and the sloping beams of light thrown
by the afternoon sun revealed a spectacle of
glittering wealth and display which is not
surpassed in any city of the world.

So thought Larkington, and so said Larkington, with that British frankness which, if
it brusquely sneers at times at American manners and solecisms, quite as freely and mag-
nanimously praises, on occasion.

" There comes the coach with the President," said one of the bachelors from the
tent; "the game will be called in five minutes. Are you ready, Larkington?" The
Englishman for answer threw off his cover
coat, and, standing revealed in his white jer-

sey, boots, and breeches, proceeded to tie
about his head a white silk *kuffia*, adjusting
it with a twisted cord, and fastening the ends
at the back of his head, after the fashion of
the Bedouins of Syria. The match on this
particular afternoon was between the bachelors and married men of the club; and as
Charles Farwell was to have played in it,
he had arranged for Larkington to take his
place.

Mrs. Fallow-Deer had begged him to do
something for the Englishman, and this had
been the easiest thing to do.

A prize cup had been offered by the ladies
of Newport, and the match was undoubtedly
the most important one of the season.

" Just like my luck to be in for this
game," Larkington had said to Stirrups that
morning.

The signal to ride into the field was now
given, and the six bachelors, chastely and ap-
propriately attired in white, rode into place at
their end of the ground. Ranged side by side,

with raised mallets, they sat waiting, their eyes fixed upon the red flag in the umpire's hand.

Their adversaries, six married men, at the opposite end of the field, were well able to cope with them, if one might judge from their appearance and that of their ponies. The figures of these men were fine and athletic; their costume was of dark blue and yellow stripes.

"Are you ready? One, two, three, go!" said the umpire; the red flag was dropped and the ball thrown into the middle of the ground.

Flash! crash! went the twelve ponies and their twelve riders, dashing toward each other at lightning speed, each and every one determined to have the first blow at the little white wooden ball, which lay peacefully on the grass.

It was a grand stroke, the first one, dealt by the mallet of a white player, who to most of the spectators was a stranger.

The ball was driven straight and clear toward the goal, and the blues had hard work in getting it back again. It was a hard-fought game, however, and both sides played well and pluckily; but the married men and their backers, who had been hopeful of success since it had been learned that Farwell, by long odds the best player of the club, was not in the field, began to be rather despondent.

Finally, after ten minutes' sharp contest, a splendid stroke from Larkington put the ball out between the two upright wands which marked the adversaries' goal, and the first game was scored by the bachelors.

Five games were played, three being won by the white players, and the Benedicts being defeated by one game.

At the close of the match Larkington was congratulated on his playing by his allies and adversaries alike, and he felt that the polo match had raised him another step in the seemingly easy ladder of American society.

Larkington called that evening at Mrs. Fallow-Deer's, and found the ladies at home.

Count Clawski, who had been dining *en famille* with Mrs. Fallow-Deer, obligingly devoted himself to her, and Larkington was left free to talk to Miss Carleton.

He was in high spirits. The splendid exercise of the afternoon had set his blood aglow, and a convivial dinner with the bachelors, which had followed at the house of their captain, had not decreased his pleasurable condition of mind and body. Miss Carleton was as charming a person to talk to, to listen to, to look at, as Larkington had ever met.

She was sitting — the attitude would be better described as reclining — in a low armchair; her strong and *svelte* young figure took a natural and thoroughly graceful pose, and the folds of her white dress fell about its outlines, revealing them, but not too distinctly for maidenliness.

Her dress, which was of some thick and soft material, was close at the neck and wrists. She had the shoulders and arms of a goddess, but she never showed them. It was one of the few bits of sentiment which her mother had never laughed her out of.

In the old days, when she and Cid had had the one-sided understanding, he had begged her to keep those beauties from the eyes of the world.

" It is enough that they can see your face," he said jealously; he would almost have liked her to wear a *yashmack*, and keep that face for his eyes alone.

She had promised him in a weak moment never to wear the undress of ball dress, and she had kept her word.

Larkington was really pleased with the beauty and grace of the girl, and, as he had written to his mother, he thought it would be an easy as well as pleasant thing to become attached to her.

He was not much used to making love to

ladies, and was not very sure of himself, but he did his best, and found that his pretty speeches were graciously, if cynically, listened to.

She puzzled him, this beauty, whose eyes did not droop, nor color change, under the ardent look of admiration which he fixed upon her.

She was thoroughly mistress of the situation, and when, after a too flagrant compliment, she turned upon him and with good-natured satire analyzed and caricatured all his speeches, cutting them to pieces, he was forced to laugh at her wit, though it had been at his own expense.

She liked his flattery, as he plainly saw, though it did not deceive her.

And when he asked if he might come to-morrow and coach her a little in her serving at tennis, which had seemed to him faulty that day at the Casino, she consented, and appointed the hour of twelve for the lesson.

"You will stay and lunch with us after the

game, Mr. Larkington?" said Mrs. Fallow-
Deer, hospitably.

"With the greatest pleasure, madam," answered the Englishman.

He took his leave. Both ladies shook
hands with him in saying good-night, — Mrs.
Fallow-Deer with the real cordiality which
underlay all the superficial artificiality of her
manner; and Gladys laid a smooth white
hand for an instant in his own.

Under similar circumstances he would
have been apt to press the hand of a woman
he so much admired, and whose manner with
him had been so easy. He was in a state of
unusual exhilaration, and even felt himself to
be a little in love.

Something, however, in the young girl's
eyes made him touch her hand as coolly and
lightly as if she had been old and ugly
instead of young and very beautiful.

There was a spirit of good-fellowship about
her that fascinated him; it alternated so
strangely with the grand air which seemed

equally natural to her, and which was as scornful and aristocratic as if she had been born a princess.

" Do you not find the American girls very different from any others, Clawski ? " he asked, as the two men left the house together.

" *Mon Dieu,* yes," replied the diplomate. " I do not pretend to understand them, and have never anything to say to them. They are to me charming, but incomprehensible. With the married women I am at home, but with the young ladies who rule so much in American society, I am quite at a loss to understand, or make myself understood."

CHAPTER IV.

GLADYS CARLETON was not one of the women who are born possessed of a demon of coquetry. The mere suffering which a man undergoes at the hands of a coquette is not in its first effects so greatly to be deprecated. It is in the consequences that lies the deepest wrong which the insincere woman does to the man who loves her. For the distrust of her whole sex which grows upon him, and the conviction that neither she nor her kind are worthy of the best that is in his nature, she is responsible. The disdain which he may feel toward her cannot greatly injure him.

But the spirit in which he regards that tendency in his nature which looks to woman for the truest support of his life, and the

systematic hardening of those qualities in
him which reach out instinctively to the
feminine side of humanity, are soul hurts,
which are not healed when the pain of the
deceived love has passed.

His judgment of the whole sex cannot
fail to be biassed by his experience of the
woman who has most deeply interested him.
Thus it is that the coquette, by lowering the
whole standard of womanhood in the eyes of
man, injures her own sex as well as the other.

The forms of coquetry are infinitely va-
ried, and some of them are much more reprehensible than others. The woman who
undertakes conquests simply for the glory of
displaying at the wheels of her chariot the
captive she holds by the rosy bonds of love,
is the commonest type.

As her coquetry is of the most patent kind,
its wounds are rarely severe or lasting, and yet
there is a certain vulgarity about this spirit of
conquest, which makes this type of women
dangerous to both men and women.

A more subtle and disastrous influence is wielded by the woman who is bent on the scientific analysis of the various effects produced by the tender passion on men of different character and nature.

She has little pigeon-holes marked with different characteristic names, and into these she classifies every new specimen. She is apt soon to discover that the pigeon-holes may be very few, and that nearly all the men she meets will fit exactly into one or another of them.

When she has arrived at this conclusion she is satisfied; two or three good specimens of every sort having been coolly analyzed and properly pigeon-holed.　　　●

It is variety, and not quantity, she desires; and, having already become quite familiar with the manner in which a certain species of the *genus homo* is affected by the greatest of passions, she allows many possible victims to pass by without an effort or desire to add them to her collection; but if a specimen hitherto unclassified crosses her path, she is ready with her little dissecting-knife to peer into the labyrinths of a new phase of human nature.

Another class, perhaps the most dangerous one, into which we are dividing coquettes, includes those women who fancy themselves in love with each fresh lover. These are emotional and sympathetic women, who, being incapable of strong feelings themselves, are borne along by the force of a passion which fascinates them, and which they would gladly reciprocate. In their often renewed disappointment at finding that the new lover cannot make them forget themselves, they feel a sense of injustice, and never dream that they are not the injured ones.

To none of these classes of coquettes did Gladys belong. She had broken her share of hearts in her day, but it was more for want of an occupation than for any other reason. She had no very particular talent

for anything, not even for society, in which
she was a prominent but not a popular
figure.

A great belle she undoubtedly was, which
did not make the women particularly fond of
her. Men all admired her, and elbowed and
fought for a place at her side in the ballroom. A good many of them were in love
with her, and yet few liked her. She was
admirable, she was lovable, but she was distinctly unlikable.

A certain fondness for the truth made her
speak it at all times, even when it carried
something of a sting with it.

Her intellect was of a high order enough
to show her the insipidity of the men and
women among whom her lot was cast. It
was not strong enough to force her to leave
the circle in which she was born, and strive
for a footing in the world of thought, action,
art, or literature.

She laughed at the Philistines, and yet
avowed herself to be one of them.

The clever men, those who wrote books and painted pictures, if they found themselves in her company, were invariably drawn toward her. She numbered a poet, two journalists, and a marine painter among her winter's conquests.

Tennis was one of her favorite amusements, and when her English acquaintance appeared, in accordance with her permission, at twelve o'clock on the morning after the polo match, he found her dressed for the game. A long practice followed, at the end of which Miss Carleton acknowledged her indebtedness to Mr. Larkington for several points.

"What can I teach you in return for your excellent coaching, Mr. Larkington?" asked Gladys, as they sat on the veranda after lunch. The young man was silent, and absently rolled himself a cigarette, using one hand in the operation, *à l'Espagnol.*

"You are silent. Does that mean that I cannot teach you anything? Well, per-

haps you are right; I am rather an ignora-
mus."

"Why do you answer your own question?
You can teach me many, many things, but
what I should like best to learn would be
how to please you, Miss Gladys."

"If you want to please me, don't call me
Miss Gladys. I am well out of my teens,
and do not care to be addressed in that
school-girl fashion. I know you have heard
other men speak of and to me in that manner; but it is an odious fashion, and I hate
it."

"I beg your pardon, Miss Carleton, — I
will not offend you again in that matter.
What are you going to do this afternoon?
You must send me away if I interfere with
any of your engagements."

"I am going out at four, in Mr. Belhomme's yacht. I want to see the sunset over
the waters. I promised my cousin, before he
left, that I would go to a certain spot and
get a particular view of the bay. I am quix-

otic in the matter of promises; yes, really
I am, and never break one. Mr. Belhomme has promised to take me just where I
want to go. Would you like to go with
us?"

"I should of course be delighted; but
would it be convenient, do you think?"

"Oh, perfectly; I make up my own party,
and invite all the people. Mrs. Fallow-Deer
is going as chaperon. I don't know how
you will like the company, I fancy you will
not know any of them; it is the Boston gang
principally."

"Indeed, I never met a Bostonian to know
him — or her. They are said to be more
like English people than New Yorkers are;
is that true?"

"Yes, I suppose it is. Those who come
to Newport are a queer lot. We have a
great many traditions about the cleverness
of the Boston women, the fascinations of the
men, but I confess to be greatly at a loss to
account for their reputation, which I don't

think is deserved. The women are not any prettier, and certainly the specimens we see here are no better informed, than the average New Yorker. They have a curious elephantine way of carrying on flirtations, which is quite peculiar to them. The men are all married and very much married; they seem to have entirely severed their relations with all womankind, save their wives. The few bachelors I have met are so petted and spoiled that there is no enduring them."

"You dispose of them in a few words."

"You shall judge if my remarks are with or without a foundation."

Before many hours passed, Mr. Larkington had an excellent opportunity of noticing the manners and customs of the " Boston gang," as Gladys had disrespectfully spoken of her guests of the afternoon.

The distance from the wharf to the great steam yacht was safely accomplished in a pretty rowboat. As soon as the party were all on board, the good yacht Dolphin steamed out of the harbor, and headed for quiet water, passing along the coast of the island, toward Providence.

Gladys, who was a capital sailor, rather viciously suggested going "outside" into the rough waters of the open sea, but she was silenced by a sharp rebuke from Mrs. Fallow-Deer, who grew pale at the very thought. The ladies of the "Boston gang" seemed no better pleased at the idea, and the Dolphin, abandoning all hopes of a tumble with the waves, cut the quiet waters evenly with her sharp prow.

Miss Carleton expatiated upon the joys of riding over the big waves.

Mr. Larkington was presented first to one and then to another of the ladies, with all of whom he found himself quite at home in a short time.

Their names he was somewhat puzzled by; many of them he had never before met with in any part of the world.

One pretty married woman with an impossible three-syllabled patronymic advised him to come to Boston for the winter, if he should remain so long in America.

She explained that for a man the Athens of America was really the most delightful place in the world. Nowhere else were they so well treated, in spite of all the talk about the rights of women.

" Things are rather reversed with us, and it is the men who have all the privileges. We women are so much in the majority that we practically have the same rights that men do. Indeed, the male sex are, in our community, the privileged class. They are exempt from every social duty, and included in every social pleasure. The charities and the reforms are carried on by ladies, who minister to the sick and uphold the privileges of the criminals. We visit the hospitals and the prisons, pay the taxes, give the parties, oversee the schools, and keep up the churches. It is a fair division, is it not?"

The lady laughed as she asked the question, and Larkington, not knowing what to answer, laughed too.

He was not quite sure whether she was in earnest or in jest. There was a certain want of softness about the voice of the lady with the three-syllabled name, a certain independence of manner, which did not please him, though he thought her pretty and bright. The pillow behind her slipped to the ground as she sat looking at the group of people at the other end of the boat. Larkington started to pick it up for her, but she had involuntarily stooped and regained it.

Then she laughed and said, —

" If Miss Carleton had dropped that pillow, it would never have occurred to her that she might pick it up. You see that I quite naturally leaned forward to get it, though you were so near me. That is the difference between the New York and Boston woman. We expect nothing from mankind; they regard the male sex as simply created for their service. Let us join the others; I think there will be some singing. Somebody has brought Miss Carleton's banjo."

The Englishman was not displeased at the opportunity thus offered of returning to that part of the deck where Gladys Carleton had thrown herself on a pile of ropes. The mast behind her served for a support. She sat in Turk fashion, a thing few women can do with comfort or with grace. At the moment when Larkington approached, Gladys was indulging in the infantile amusement of playing ball with Mr. Silsbee Saltonstall, of Boston. A red apple provided by the steward served for the plaything.

Mr. Saltonstall was a good-looking young fellow of eight and twenty, tall, rather gracefully modelled, with a decidedly handsome head. His was an earnest face, with deep blue near-sighted eyes, blond beard, a wide forehead, and peculiarly sparkling white teeth.

Gladys threw the apple in the most provoking manner, trying every time to toss it out of his reach, but Saltonstall had not played in the Harvard Base Ball Nine for nothing, and he caught it every time, making impossible reaches in all directions.

After a few minutes, Gladys wearied of the game, and tossed the apple overboard " for the fishes," she said.

Then Saltonstall, in obedience to a half-gesture from the girl, took his place beside her on an adjacent pile of ropes.

Gladys did not look at Larkington, who stood near by, but began talking seriously and in a rather low voice to the Bostonian.

" Your sister tells me you are writing a book, Mr. Saltonstall, on the higher ethics of sociology. I was much interested in talking to her about it. I fancy you do not agree with Herbert Spencer in all his premises, from what I know of your character."

" You are quite right, Miss Carleton. I find that, in working out to a logical conclusion the principles which Spencer advances, one finds one's self in a *cul-de-sac*, and is led up to a blind wall. I therefore maintain that certain of his premises, and the inferences he draws from them, are fallacious. In my book I have tried to explain my doubts of his principles."

" How interesting you must find it to set your mind in an antagonistic attitude to thinkers like Spencer and Huxley! Could you explain to me just where you differ from these English philosophers ? "

" In the hypothesis which they maintain concerning cerebral action and intellectual activity. Morality and immorality, according to Huxley, depend merely upon the condition of the muscles and tissues of the body. He admits no responsibility of man, save towards his descendants. For his own misdeeds man is not responsible ; his sins are chargeable to the account of society. The inner essence, the ideal side of human nature, is denied. But let us talk of something else besides my hobbies, Miss Carleton.

I see I am boring you already, and I have driven your English friend away from your side in terror and amaze."

" And why should you assume that you are boring me, Mr. Saltonstall?   Do you think me incapable of following your conversation ? "

" Not for an instant, Miss Carleton ; it is not that you could not think, and think intelligently, upon this subject, or any other that I could talk to you about — only — I do not think, to speak frankly, that it interests you."

" Then why should I have begun by speaking of it ? "

" Your natural goodness of heart prompted you to try to put me at my ease."

" You have known me long enough to know that I have n't any natural goodness of heart."

" Politeness, then.   You will acknowledge that you have that quality to an uncommon degree ? "

" Prevarication. Pure prevarication this, Mr. Saltonstall. It is quite useless to pursue it with me. Remember that I have known you a very long time, and though our acquaintance has been a superficial one, still it has given me some chances to judge of your character. Dissimulation is not a natural weakness of yours. You have, no doubt, quite enough sins without cultivating that one. Take my advice and remain the living curiosity that you are, the one man who is not a liar. Now tell me why a cloud came into your eyes suddenly, and you shrouded the thoughts in which I was becoming so deeply interested. Frankly now — tell me."

" If you will have the truth, Miss Carleton, I have a particular and possibly unreasonable objection to submitting myself to the process known among ladies as ' drawing a man out.' I distinctly dislike to be made to ride my hobby around a lady's drawing-room, or even around her yacht."

"And why do you think I was drawing you out?"

"Because you are aware that a man is never so agreeably employed as when expounding his own particular theory to an indulgent listener."

"In other words, you imagine that I was martyrizing myself by listening to your talk, in order that I might inspire you with the pleasant impression that you had succeeded in interesting me?"

"Yes."

"From what source have you drawn these conclusions?"

"From my former experience of the fair sex. A man may be flattered even when he is not deceived, Miss Carleton. It is a source of satisfaction to know that one has aroused a desire to please."

"You flatter yourself too much in this case, in fancying that I would take the trouble to counterfeit an interest I do not feel, to act a part, for your benefit."

" It is hardly an effort to follow the dictates of one's nature, Miss Carleton."

" And you imply exactly what ? "

" That the love of conquest is fixed in the feminine character. It is the old fable of the knight and the witch. ' The love of power' is the answer to the feminine riddle."

" I really ought to be angry at your impertinence, I suppose. But a soft answer turneth away wrath. I will rather try to convince you of the error of your ways. Women are by nature sympathetic. That natural sympathy of temperament is touched not only on the emotional side, but also on the intellectual. They have thinking-machines which are for the most part kept quite idle, — without ' feed,' to use a mechanical simile. The new thoughts which a man may bring them quickly set the thinking-machine in motion, and it eagerly draws the 'feed' into its interior. Your hobby is to another man who has a stable full of his own, a bore and a nuisance ; to a woman who is hobbyless, it is sometimes the greatest pleasure to go for a gallop *en croupe* behind a gallant rider who bestrides a well-groomed hobby. Now I was in mid gallop over a new road, familiar to you, interesting to me, when the hobby, being well bred, does not stumble, but the man does, and down we all come together, dissatisfied and balked of our ride. The stone in the road which upset us being nothing in the world but the suspicion — vanity — how shall I call that quality in the Boston man which is so individual, so intangible, so utterly exasperating ? "

" You cannot expect me to help you to find that word which is to condemn myself."

" I have it — caution."

" Miss Carleton, if a man would keep his peace of mind, he must hold fast to caution in your society."

" Why ? "

" Because your fascinations are so devastating to future security and peace."

" Then you would rather not be fascinated ?

Strange creature! A European would look
on you as a lunatic. And yet it is the characteristic of your race. One would almost
fancy you to be like the youth in the song
of Heine, who, when the beautiful maiden
asks him the source of his grief, replies:
'I belong to that race of Asras who must
die when they love.' But, to convince you
that I have no design in 'drawing you out,'
to prove that I am not plotting against your
peace of mind, I shall join the Philistines,
who have been clamoring for a song; will
you help me in the chorus?"

Saltonstall could not sing, unfortunately,
and he rather unreasonably resented the
breaking up of a *tête-à-tête* so agreeable, so
dangerous. Gladys tuned her banjo, and, a
mandolin being found in the depths of Mr.
Belhomme's stateroom, Larkington accompanied the music of the tinkling instrument
with the softer picking of the mandolin
strings. He had learned to play the instrument in Naples long ago, he said. The girl

had a strong, sweet soprano voice; the man, a baritone of velvety quality.

They first sang the popular music of the time, the strains of Iolanthe and the Sorcerer. Then, as the day waned and the sea and sky grew rosy and golden with the sunset colors, they sang tender Italian folksongs.

Saltonstall stood leaning against the mast, looking at Gladys as she stood facing him, her figure in a pose of perfect grace, her head thrown back a little, her white hands touching the strings of her instrument. Her face was lit up with the warm hues of the sunset clouds; behind her was a background of dark land and gray sky.

As the boat glided smoothly along the shores of the island, the mighty trees of Redwood loomed up, looking twice their size in the uncertain light. Over the tops of the proud trees crept the big yellow moon slowly, flooding the heavens with her light, shaming the garish fires of the western sky.

As they entered the harbor and drew near the wharf, the two voices, which had for a time been silent, broke forth into a "good-night," — a pretty German serenade, which was received with great applause.

"Thank you for the most perfect day of my life," whispered Larkington, as he helped Gladys down the gangway to the little boat.

"Good-night and good-by, Miss Carleton," said Silsbee Saltonstall. "I shall not have the pleasure of seeing you again, as I leave Newport to-morrow."

"And has to-day been so long that the month you yesterday expected to pass at Newport seems to have gone by? Thank you for the compliment. Good-by; *bon voyage.* Take my advice, and, as you are a cautious Boston man, don't go to Mt. Desert. I should recommend the Adiron-dacks for you. Good-night."

True to his word, Silsbee Saltonstall left Newport the next morning. He felt himself on the verge of falling in love with the strange girl with the deep eyes and lovely voice. It was not in accordance with his plan of life to fall in love for the next ten years.

He followed Miss Carleton's advice in avoiding Mount Desert, and chose instead a month's camping out in Northern Maine. The sonnet he wrote to her that night after the sail Gladys never saw till years after, when she stumbled upon it in a book of his verses.

CHAPTER V.

On Monday evening all the *beau monde* of Newport assemble and meet together in the hall, or theatre, of the Casino.

It is a pretty building, with wide-roofed piazzas running around it on two sides. There are delicious corners and angles in these piazzas, where confidences may be whispered, and protestations might be made, if anybody had time to make protestations at Newport during the season.

The hall is a large apartment, with a stage at one end. The walls are of a pretty light tint, and the gallery with its rounded arches is of a graceful design. The polished hardwood floor is cleared on Monday evening for dancing.

On the evening in question, the hall was filled with an unusually large company of gayly dressed people. Every available seat was occupied, and the crowd of black coats in the doorways was as dense as it is at a Boston Papanti party. The corresponding number of pretty, fresh, unattended young girls on the benches was not, however, to be found.

The hum of the voices was very loud, almost deafening to a silent person when the sound was not drowned by the music. At the right-hand upper corner of the room the talk seemed to be the loudest. Here sat a group of people conversing busily and earnestly. This little knot of eighteen or twenty persons included those whom Gladys had yclept the " Boston gang." The central figure was that of a tall handsome lady, with a loud voice and brusque manner.

" I call it very shabby of Mrs. Fallow-Deer to leave me out of the hunt dinner; but it 's a comfort to know that none of the rest of you are goin'," said the handsome brusque lady.

" It was just like her, but I suppose Gladys Carleton was at the bottom of it. Were the invitations given out in Mrs. Fallow-Deer's name ? "

The speaker was the lady with the three-syllabled name whom Larkington had met on board the Dolphin on the occasion of the yachting party.

" No," said the handsome brusque lady; " but everybody knows that she and Gray Grosvenor made out the list. As to Gladys Carleton, I can't say I blame her for not likin' Boston people."

" Why ? " asked several voices.

" Because, when she came on there to make a visit last winter, she had a perfectly horrid time. She stayed with some people livin' on Newbury Street, whom she had met in Europe. They were from Philadelphia, and nobody knew them in Boston, though they had lived there five years. I got her an invitation to the assembly, but she would not go because her friends were not asked. They were very nice people, but somehow they did not 'get on' in Boston."

"Don't you think that the Hub is a pretty hard place for any stranger to 'get on' in?"

Mr. Curtis Sears was the speaker. He was a young Bostonian, with a cold thoughtful face, who looked as if he had been fed on ice-water during his infancy, instead of the less chilly fluid provided by nature for the human young. His question was answered by the handsome brusque lady.

"Yes, Mr. Sears, I quite agree with you. A stranger who comes to Boston for a few weeks, if he brings proper letters, is sure to receive a great deal of attention. We like a lion immensely. But with people who come to live amongst us, it is a very different matter. Then it is not a question of an acquaintanceship of a few weeks, but a permanent one. That makes such a difference."

"One of my old classmates at college married last year, and brought his wife, who was a New York belle, to Boston. She hap-

pened to have neither relatives nor friends in
our city, and as he was little given to society,
he had few personal relations with it. He
belonged to one of the best families, but that
served the little bride in no wise. People
simply let her alone. A few of the best-
mannered of the neighbors called upon her,
and the husband's relatives asked her to dine
once at their several houses, and 'there it
stopped. She now rails against Boston, and
lives but in the hope of inducing her husband to remove to New York."

"The truth of the matter is," said the
pretty lady with the three-syllabled name,
"that we don't want all the nice men to
marry out of Boston. We all have cousins
and sisters, even if our daughters are too
young to think about from a matrimonial
standpoint, and it is very aggravating to
have these New York women just pick and
choose all our best matches, while we are
groaning under the overwhelming surplus of
our female population."

This remark was received by the ladies of the "gang" with a noticeable warmth and sympathy.

At this moment a group of people entered the ballroom, attracting the attention of all its occupants.

"These are the people from the hunt dinner," said the handsome lady.

The gentlemen of the party of new arrivals — there were perhaps fifteen of them — were dressed in red evening coats and white breeches. The costumes of the ladies were all pretty, and bore enough resemblance to each other to make the whole company appear to be in uniform. Mrs. Fallow-Deer, leaning on the arm of Mr. Belhomme, headed the train. In her hand she carried a long polo mallet of flowers. Mrs. Craig bore on her arm a saddle of pansies. Gladys Carleton, who entered the room last with Mr. Larkington, had been awarded, as a floral token from the dinner, a hunting-horn of scarlet flowers, which she wore over her shoulder, attached by a red ribbon. The entrance of the gay party was a picturesque and striking feature of the evening.

Their arrival seemed to brighten up the company already assembled, the hum of talk grew louder, and the crowd of dancers thicker than it had been earlier in the evening. The band was playing the wavy, intoxicating music of Strauss, and the circling couples danced rhythmically to the measures of the slow waltz.

" Will you dance with me, Miss Carleton ? " asked Larkington.

" No, Mr. Larkington ; I am not in the mood for dancing to-night. You should ask Mrs. Craig ; she is an excellent dancer. I am too blue to care about waltzing."

" How can you say that you are blue when you have been the life of the dinner? You never looked more brilliantly well than to-night. Has anything annoyed you, — have I — "

" You flatter yourself too highly, Mr.

Larkington. No, nothing has happened, and you have nothing to do with my indigo fit."

"Something has — "

Gladys again interrupted her interlocutor. "No, nothing has! I am simply tired of myself. There is the difficulty. You know something of the ways of people; have you ever before known a person in my position, with plenty to eat and drink, good clothes to wear, kind friends, and perfect health, who was perfectly weary of herself? It is not life that I am bored with, but myself. I am so tired of my own face that I cannot bear to look in the glass; as to my inner self, it is the most tiresome, utterly uninteresting thing to me in the wide world."

"I cannot understand your state of mind, Miss Gladys, — I beg pardon, I forgot, — Miss Carleton. Is it not Newport that you are bored with? Why not try some other place for a change?"

"Why? I cannot leave myself behind, no

matter how fast I might travel, seeking new scenes, from Mt. Desert to Saratoga."

The Englishman looked mildly bewildered and answered nothing; gazing, meanwhile, straight into the deep eyes which knew no shadow of turning. He was certainly falling in love — perhaps he had already fallen in love — with this original, many-sided creature, as fascinating to him as she was incomprehensible. Larkington had steadily persisted in his attentions to Miss Carleton, and was not ashamed to have it known that he was her devoted admirer. He avoided making the acquaintance of other ladies as much as possible; and when he could not be at her side in society, he would stand alone, watching her every movement. The sort of cowardice which Gladys had found in some of her compatriot lovers, who endeavored to screen their admiration of her from the world, had no place in the actions of the Englishman. He waited for her every morning when she drove out for shopping or visit-

ing in her cousin Amelia's pretty cart with
the Carleton crest on harness and trappings.
He followed on horseback, meeting her at
every turn. In the afternoon he was always
in attendance, even if there were other men
about, and in society she was the only woman
under fifty with whom he ever exchanged a
remark.

This absolute devotion was rather attractive to Gladys. She was amused by the big,
handsome man who was so entirely of the
world worldly, in most respects, and yet
seemed so perfectly unaccustomed to the
ways of women.

He had a fund of interesting experiences
to relate, and, being gifted with a powerful
imagination and a vivid faculty of description, he was never at a loss for an anecdote
of travel or adventure.

His stories of life in Australia were thrill-
ing and full of crisp humor. He knew
Russia and the other northern countries of
Europe, as well as the more frequented

southern lands. What he knew he had
learned from actual contact with the world
and its people, and there was no guide-book
knowledge or other cheap information to be
got from him. He had lived in Syria with
a band of Bedouins, and his descriptions of
their adventurous life never failed to interest
Gladys. He had learned their strange music, and could sing their wild songs of love
and battle wonderfully well. He had no
theories about the men and women he had
known. They had fallen across his path like
people one meets in the glare of mid-day,
when no shadow is cast upon the ground
by the figures. He saw them clean cut,
as they stood against the background of
their own surroundings, and no shadowy
reflection fell behind them as his explanation of their characters or actions. He saw
people distinctly, and remembered them as
they were. This quality of impersonal judgment was very fascinating to Gladys, who always enveloped the men and women she had

known in a sort of misty garment of her own imaginings, which blurred their real outlines.

"If you will not dance, Miss Carleton, will you not come out on the piazza during the waltz, it is so very warm here?"

"By all means; let us go."

The two young people, whose names were already linked together by the busybodies of Newport, left the hot ballroom and passed out into the cool evening air. It is never hot at night in Newport. The sea-breeze sweeps across the island, refreshing those who have suffered the terrible heats of the city summer, and have come to the fresh health-giving climate for rest.

On the wide piazza groups of men were sitting together, talking and smoking, or silently enjoying the beauty of the perfect summer night.

In one of the shadowy corners stood two chairs lately vacated by Mrs. Craig and Count Clawski. Gladys placed herself in one of these, her companion seating himself at her side.

" Now tell me things," said the girl, imperatively.

" What shall it be about to-night? "

" Oh! anything you like. You might finish telling me about the Bedouin chief who fell in love with the English lady."

" No, that is rather too long a story. May I not tell you something about Newport and what has happened to me since I first met you here in this very Casino? "

" Decidedly not. That would be quite too commonplace and every-day an experience."

Larkington was silent and meditatively stroked his moustache, from which action he seemed to derive a certain comfort.

As they sat quite silent, a light flashed close to the face of Gladys, — a tiny golden spark, — and was quickly lost again in the darkness.

" What a pretty firefly, and how bright! "

" You should take the firefly as your device, Miss Carleton, for it resembles you more than anything else that I have seen."

" If it is a compliment, thank you kindly. You know I like pretty speeches as well as Mrs. Craig likes *bonbons*. But exactly *why* am I like a firefly? I have no wings."

" In the song about Zuleika's eyes which you liked, they are compared to the light of the firefly. When they are turned upon her lover all is bright and beautiful, but when the lids drop before their light, like the wings of the firefly, the world is dark."

"Did you ever know any one called Zuleika?"

"Yes."

" Where did she live? "

" In a little tent near the banks of the river Jordan."

"Was she pretty? "

" Hardly pretty; the term is too English to describe the black-browed Zuleika."

" Who was she ? "

" The daughter of the sheik Abdul, with whom I lived some time."

" But how was it possible that you should

know, or even see, his daughter? Is not that against the law of Mohammedan etiquette?"

"Yes. It happened strangely enough. Zuleika, you must know, spoke English, and was, among her people, a marvel of learning. It happened in this wise. The Bedouin who fell in love with the English lady, a brother of Abdul's, finally left his tribe, gave up his wives, and married Lady Margaret Hopeston, an eccentric woman with a large fortune. They lived in Damascus, this strangely matched couple, and led, it is said, an extremely happy life. One morning Lady Margaret was roused at an early hour by the sound of a cavalcade tramping in her courtyard. On descending to ascertain the reason for the commotion, her eyes were greeted by a strange sight. A whole band of Bedouins, several hundred in number, were crowded into the courtyard and lower story of the house. They were the tribe of her husband, who, having been worsted in battle and pursued by a hostile band, had come to take refuge within his gates, in the city of Damascus. For a week the whole band claimed the hospitality of their brother, and made their camp in the house and grounds of Lady Margaret. Her attention was attracted to Abdul, then young and handsome (he has often assured me) as the morning star, tall as the palm-tree, and strong as the whirlwind. Abdul was at that time in great trouble; his favorite wife had died, leaving him the one daughter of his house, Zuleika, then a child of five. Instead of intrusting her to the care of the women, Abdul was always with the little girl, who was as dear to him as the spring of water in the desert. Lady Margaret was struck by the devotion of this young father to his child, and became deeply interested in the pair. When the welcome time came for the departure of her strange guests, Lady Margaret asked of Abdul his daughter, his Zuleika, the breath of his body, the sun of his sky. It was all she asked of him, and he, the sheik of the tribe, could refuse no request made by the woman who had sheltered his people. 'I gave my Zuleika to the wife of my brother — to the woman with great learning — without a tear without a sigh.' I remember the way in which Abdul told me this, as if it were but yesterday. We were sitting on the sand outside the tent, a great fire blazing before us. Some of the men of the tribe were dancing one of their wild barbaric war dances on the other side of the fire. The light gleamed on their naked swords, their dark fierce faces, and the white drapery of their burnooses. It was a scene never to be forgotten. Zuleika remained with Lady Margaret and learned many things which were of use to her in after life. First of all, Lady Margaret taught her the English language. Zuleika's new friend showed much common-sense in her education of the girl. She knew that it would be impossible to make an English woman of her, and so, beyond the habits of

cleanliness, and the arts of sewing and cooking, she made no attempt to anglicize the
little maiden. Zuleika was taught to em-
broider the beautiful patterns you value so
much in this country. I have a scarf she
worked for me, which I will show you some
time. For seven years the daughter of Abdul remained the constant companion of
Lady Margaret, but at the end of that time
the restlessness which had ever been upon
her grew too great to bear. She was a
woman now, according to the reckoning of
her people, and the life of restriction had
never been pleasant to her. She fled away
in the night to the desert, where 'she heard
the stars calling her,' and with the help of
one of her people found her father. Abdul
rejoiced at the return of the daughter he had
mourned as one dead, and kept her always
near him. Her condition was a pitiable
one. Her father had not the heart to force
her to marry among his people, for the
girl was naturally intelligent, and with the

education she had received, rebelled at the thought of being linked to a savage. Another time I will tell you how I came to cast my lot with Abdul the Sheik; it is a long history of adventure which you may find interesting. It is enough now to say that for three months I was his guest. At that time I was quite ignorant of Arabic, though I soon learned enough to make myself understood. Zuleika, summoned by her father from the tent of the women, would serve as an interpreter between my host and myself, and during the evenings when we sat together smoking before the tent door, the girl would stand at Abdul's side, and translate to him all the things he so eagerly asked of me. He was peculiarly intelligent, and had learned from his daughter much concerning European customs and character. He was never tired of hearing about England and the manner of warfare practised by the English. In return for what I could tell him, the sheik would recite to me the traditions of his tribe, and sing the songs of his nation. Zuleika, as you will imagine, added much to the interest of these conversations, telling me of her strange life with Lady Margaret, and the terrible gulf which it had made between herself and her people. What a long story! and how tired you must be! Have you heard enough about Zuleika?" Larkington asked.

"No, not half enough! But there is Mrs. Fallow-Deer, looking for me. I suppose I must go. You may come to-morrow evening and tell me the rest of your romance of Arabia. Good-night."

CHAPTER VI.

Much that is best worth seeing in New-port is never seen by a majority of the people who visit the town during "the season." In the eighteen miles length and nine miles breadth of the island are many nooks and grottos unknown to those individuals who limit their expedition to the ocean drive, and the path across the beaches. Artists know these spots and linger in them. Lovers find them out somehow instinctively. But Newport has now become the resort of the rich, and even the dwellers in the quiet country farm-houses demand exorbitant prices for their simple accommodations. So artists are rarely met with, and, as it has been hinted, there are few people who take time at this most brilliant of watering-places to fall in love.   Love-Lane, Fairy Dell, Glen Anna, Vaucluse, and Lawton's Valley have few visitors.

It is a pity that the worldlings have found out this region of delight.   Any other place would have served as well for the display of their horses and carriages, diamonds, clothes, beauty, and beaux.   Why should they have chosen to erect their palatial cottages on our quiet island, to pass their idle summer in the quaint old town?

The love of nature is not always a natural gift.   With the dwellers in cities, the taste is usually one which has been acquired through the influence of some country-bred or poetic mind.   How many beauties of sky and woodland, flower and tree, has not Wordsworth taught us to see?   Keats has led thousands of ears to note the music in the wild bird's carol, which else had hardly heeded it.   Who does not see a new delight in the simple field flower after reading Burns's description of the daisy?

The love of what is beautiful in art is oftener found with the dwellers of a city than the appreciation of those beauties in nature which art reflects. The person who is deeply impressed by a fine landscape painting will often pass by the view which inspired the painter without observing its qualities of color and effects of light and shade. The sensitive woman who shrinks at the well-depicted portrait of a wretched beggar will pass the poor creature whose misery has struck the artist without a pang of pity. The girl who weeps bitterly over the sorrows of a heroine in a novel watches with more amusement than sympathy the grief and trials of the heroine of a life romance.

Gladys Carleton had a good knowledge of art and its laws. A bad picture set her teeth on edge, and she could go through an art gallery without a catalogue, and tell the name of every painter whose work hung before her. With nature she was not so much at home, though a new understanding seemed to be gradually coming to her of its secrets and charms. It was not without a certain pain that this new feeling crept about her, — it seemed to be a part of the grieved loneliness which she had lately experienced.

"People can be nothing to us; there is nothing which can stand by us but our work, and when we have not any work, we are alone."

The speech was not a very coherent one, and the person to whom it was addressed received it in silence.

"Books are a help, but it is so one-sided a friendship one has with one's book friends. We cannot answer, and only receive, never giving anything in return for what we get from them."

Gladys Carleton was the speaker, and the listener, Larkington, her faithful cavalier.

"You live too much with your books, Miss Carleton, and too little with your kind. It makes you melancholy. You should learn to care more for people and less for ideas."

"What nonsense you are talking, Mr. Larkington! Excuse me for plain speaking, but you are, really. I do not think you understand at all what I mean."

"I fear that I do not."

There was a pause, after which Gladys said abruptly, —

"How far is it to the sea?"

"About half a mile, I fancy."

"Please go down to the shore and bring me a piece of red seaweed."

"I cannot leave you here alone."

"Why not, if I order you to go? Do you not know how to be obedient?"

"You are teaching me, Miss Carleton. I never knew before that it was pleasanter to obey than to be obeyed."

"Of course it is. There is no such luxury in the world as self-abnegation; it is the thing we all long for."

"I do not fancy that you would enjoy it; you are too imperious by nature. You were born to command. I never heard you make a request in your life."

"In other words, you think me a bully? Now go this instant! I won't have you stay here and abuse me. *Go*, I say, and bring me the bunch of red seaweed."

"You are cruel, but I yield. You are not afraid to be left alone?"

"No; I am within calling distance from the house."

When she was alone, the tall beauty rose from her seat on the trunk of a fallen tree, and walked rapidly in the opposite direction. The path over which she passed was fragrant with pine needles and wild flowers. Overhead hung the boughs of the larch-trees which lined the walks, and over the trees was the soft blue of the summer sky. Carrying her riding crop in one hand, and holding her habit with the other, she ran down the path, which sloped suddenly toward the great pond at its foot.

Gladys had ridden out to visit a country friend, who lived in a quiet vale many miles distant from the gay town. Finding her friend absent, the girl and the admirer, who had been privileged to ride with her, had left their horses in charge of the groom, and walked down to view the quiet beauty of the vale. Gladys loved the place, and was not in the mood for badinage with Larkington. She wished to be alone, and so had sent him off in quest of the bunch of red seaweed. She had not been in this pleasant spot for many years. She remembered the last time she had visited it. Cid had been with her. The thought of him had made the presence of the Englishman hateful to her.

At the edge of the pond the path swerved to the left, leading down to the deep gorge below. A narrow ledge of rock stretched to the right, skirting the millpond, a precipice of a hundred feet yawning on one side, the deep water on the other. With a quick step the girl passed along the narrow rocky ledge, and seated herself on a great stone, which lay just where the black sheet of water poured smoothly over the edge of the dam, to be frothed into a white mass of foam at the bottom of the fall. A strong young willow-tree behind the rock served her as a support, and, twining one arm about its slender stem, she sat overhanging the waterfall, looking down into the deep pool.

The bare hand which embraced the trunk touched a rough surface, and her fingers traced the outline of some letters, cut into the bark. She could not see the letters, they were on the other side of the tree, but she had not forgotten the day when they were carved, all those years ago, — G. C. and C. F., with a true lover's knot between the initials. She laid her cheek against the willow and sat quite silent, looking down, always down, into the black pool at her feet. The downcast eyelids quivered and let fall a tear, which dropped unnoted on her knee. Another and another drop of nature's balm coursed down the pale cheek, and the chest. trembled with emotion of a silent weeping. There was no violence,

nothing of that tearing grief with which the
women who have lived, loved, and suffered
weep out the agony which seems like to rend
body and soul apart. The burden of her
life seemed too great for her to bear, and she
wept for the emptiness of her lot, of her
heart. A verse from a poem which had
always seemed appropriate to herself ran
through her mind : —

> " Elle est morte, et n'a point vécu ;
> Elle faisait semblant de vivre.
> De ses mains est tombé le livre
> Dans lequel elle n'a rien lu."

When she was dead, what so appropriate as
this poem, " Sur une Morte," of De Musset's,
could be read over her cold clay? Why
should she not die now? How easy would
it be to slip down from the great rock,
and lose herself in the oblivion of the black
pool, with the white foam dancing above
her? " Who would care much ? " she
asked herself, and answered her own question with more tears. No one would really

miss her. Her mother would grieve a little while, but the other daughters would soon receive the share of affection which the shallow parent had given her. It was a love of offspring only, and had no tie of sympathy to deepen it.

How easy it would be to move a few steps to the edge of the great stone, to lean far over the abyss, holding on by the tree, and at last to let go her grasp and fall through the soft air to the cool black water, then one great pain — and afterwards, rest! There was the terrible thought — if it should not be rest which she should find beneath the dancing foam bubbles.

Was it that thought only which kept her from doing the thing which she had pictured to herself? Was it the doubt which held her back? "Yes," she reasoned, "only that. Were we but sure of what awaits us on the other side, how many of us would remain upon the hither bank of the dark river which men call death, and which saints believe leads to life everlasting."

She crept nearer to the edge, and, still clasping the tree with both arms, leaned over the rushing torrent. How easy it would be! One little movement and all would be over. The slender fingers closely clasped about the tree were all that steadied her. If she should suddenly unlace them the movement would throw her off her balance — and the great riddle would be solved. Why should she not? Was it all a jest? Was she in earnest or in jest? She did not know.

She was fascinated by the strange thought, and stood swaying over the verge of the dizzy height, intoxicated with the danger. In one instant she could regain a firm footing on the ledge, or — what was the trembling she felt beneath her feet? Was there an earthquake? Ah! with a wild cry, it was the rock under her feet that shook. It had become loosened by her weight on its extreme edge, it swayed one instant, and in the next must be dashed into the boiling caldron below — and she?

This was her reward for trifling with the

great power.   Death, whom she had thought about so lightly, had now come to claim her grimly.   She looked up into the blue sky, which was so fair, and out over the beauty of the lonely gorge.   She felt, as she had never done before, the beauty about her on every side.   She saw the possibilities of happiness and usefulness which she had so utterly neglected.   She knew that life was a blessing, and in the cry which startled the still air there was remorse for her thanklessness as well as agony for her danger.

The rock thrilled once more beneath her, and as it trembled 'twixt the ledge and the precipice, Gladys lifted a prayer for her life to the God whose existence she had some time denied.

A strong hand clasped her fingers, she felt her waist firmly seized, and in an instant she knew that she was safe, though the great rock had fallen from its bed with a mighty crash, and the white foam was dashed upon her check and brow.   She was carried a few steps in a pair of strong arms which pressed her close to a fast-beating heart. She was placed gently on a mossy bank by some one who spoke no word. Her eyes were closed, though she had not fainted, and she knew whose arm had saved her in the hour of danger. She was grateful and looked up to speak.

The face into which she glanced was deadly white, and the eyes were dim. She rose to her feet, for he looked so strangely. As she stood up strong, though trembling slightly, the man at her side reeled, as if he had been struck, and fell fainting to the ground at her feet.

The girl knew quite well what to do, and, being one of those persons who are never overcome by an emergency, she quickly brought the swooning man to his senses. A copious sprinkling with cold water and the application of Miss Carleton's vinaigrette to his nostrils caused Mr. Cuthbert Larkington to open his eyes in a few moments. When he was quite restored, Gladys, turning her face from him, said, —

"You have saved my life — and I am very grateful to you! May I ask you a great favor?"

"Need you doubt it?"

"It is this, that you will never mention what has happened to-day to any one. Promise me. Do not even speak of it to me. I cannot bear to think of it. It was too terrible."

"Yes, I will promise on one condition."

"And that is?"

"That you will swear to me never to risk your precious life again so wilfully, so wickedly."

"It should be a precious life?"

"It is dearer to me than my own."

"Well, I promise. Now pledge me your word."

She held out to him her delicate hand, white as snow, pink as apple blossoms. The man touched it with his own strong fingers.

The contact seemed to move him strangely. His pale face flushed, and, clasping the dainty hand, he kissed it a score of times on wrist and fingers and rosy palm.

"I forgive you because you did me the favor to help me out of a very perilous position just now. But remember that is why you are pardoned. I shall ask you to ride to town alone. My groom will lead my horse; and I will drive in with my friends to-morrow. I mean to ask a night's shelter at the vale; I am hardly equal to the ride."

"Let me go to town and fetch out a carriage for you."

"Thank you, no. I cannot go back, to-night, to all the noise and glare of Newport. It is so peaceful here."

"You have not inquired whether my quest of the seaweed was successful. Here is the little crimson ocean flower."

"Thank you so much; I had forgotten all about it. That is a beautiful specimen. Do you feel quite yourself again?"

" Yes. It was awfully soft of me to faint in that way; I am thoroughly ashamed of myself. Do you despise me for it?"

" No. After you had saved me you had a right to be terrified. Had you been frightened before, I should not have been here now. Are you glad you saved me?"

" Do you not know —"

" Oh yes, of course I know," said the girl hastily, interrupting his vehemence; "and I am glad, too."

She turned and looked at the place where she had so lately stood in mortal danger. Everything was peaceful and quiet now. The cool plash of the water came to her ears, and the tender song of a wild bird fell like a triumphant hymn of praise upon the stillness of the day.

" It is good to live," said the song of the bird.

" It is enough to be a little part of such a world," sighed the girl. "Why cannot we forget ourselves and our petty ambitions, our loves and our hates, in the peace of all this beauty?"

She spoke half to herself and half to the bird. Larkington knew that he was not addressed. He felt a terrible sense of loneliness. He was with the woman he loved, close at her side. He had carried her in his arms but now, and yet she was farther from him at that moment than she had ever seemed before.

With the feeling of this distance there came to him a great pain unknown before. What it meant he could not know. If one had told him, he could not have understood the words. He suffered dumbly, ignorantly, with a new sense of his capacity for suffering.

Poor wretch! Miserable sham, impostor, and liar,—false to all men and women, false to himself; in that keen suffering awoke within him the soul which had till now slept.

CHAPTER VII.

THE morning of the great Newport picnic
dawned bright and clear, and the hearts of
all the happy people who were privileged to
join the exclusive and aristocratic affair were
much lighter than they had been on the previous evening, when the weather looked very
dubious. No heart so light, though, as that
of Mr. Gray Grosvenor, the prime mover in
the picnic, — the man in whose brain the
idea had at first originated, broadened, and
finally emerged in the complete and perfect
plan.

Mr. Gray Grosvenor was a very prominent
man in Newport society, — more prominent
than Mr. Belhomme, though he was not
nearly so rich. He was more courted even
than Mrs. Fallow-Deer, though he "did

not entertain," and her hospitable doors were opened every day in the week to some guest or guests.

Larkington, now well established in society by his month's stay in Newport, had quickly seen that Gray Grosvenor was a man to whom, for some reason, every one was extremely deferential and polite. He was evidently a man to be treated with great consideration; and the Englishman had taken the cue, though what claims this gentleman had to an over-punctilious politeness from society he had been at a loss to discover. He danced wonderfully well; that, of course, made him popular with the ladies; but then there were others who tripped as lightly the measures of Terpsichore, and had withal figures more suited to the graceful waltz than was the stout and roundabout body of Mr. Gray Grosvenor.

Larkington had asked Mrs. Craig confidentially to tell him all about this gentleman, by whom he had been considerably

which is snobbery, the other vanity, you
must give up all hopes of entering the inner
circle of Hades, — for which read society.
He is the man who can cut your name from
the list of a subscription ball, can keep you
out of any club he belongs to, if he happens
not to fancy the cut of your dress-coat or
the way you wear your moustache.   He

holds, beside this, another position, — that of a sort of gentleman caterer. It is a unique office, I think. He gets up all the assemblies, and arranges the *menu* of the supper, as well as the list of subscribers. He is willing to do this sort of work for society, and on the whole society is grateful to him, as no one else would give the time, pains, and trouble to it. Though he is in a sense the servant of society, inasmuch as he serves it, he is also its ruler, and he is courted from fear, if from nothing else, like the French king with the little leaden images in his hat. Gray Grosvenor's images are of gold, and not of lead."

"One sees that you do not like the gentleman, Mrs. Craig?" said Larkington.

"Like him? Why should I? Because I come from Baltimore, and he does n't happen to know anything about me, he leaves me out of his picnic. I not only dislike him, but I have been praying solemnly for the last week that it might rain on the day fixed for his fête, and spoil it all."

Count Clawski, who was in these days the devoted slave of the pretty Mrs. Craig, joined the two, who were sitting where we first saw them, in the long balcony of the Casino.

" You are speaking of the picnic, madam," said the diplomate, whose calm and punctilious manner was for the nonce upset. He looked angry and excited. " *Parbleu*, I will not go, if it rains or shines."

" I heard you had ordered a wonderful *vol-au-vent* at Hartman's for your contribution," said Mrs. Craig.

" He asks me, this man," continued the Count, notwithstanding Mrs. Craig's remarks, " to subscribe for his picnic, to bring a dish, and a bottle of wine; and when I say to him, ' Now, I will a lady with me bring,' he says, ' Excuse me, I must ask you to send her name in for the approval of the committee!' Committee indeed! I never heard of any but that of Mr. Gray Grosvenor himself; it is to me an insult. Should I bring

any lady that he or his committee might not
be proud to receive? "

Notwithstanding the prayers of Mrs. Craig,
the day of the picnic, as has been said,
dawned bright and clear.

Gladys · Carleton, as she stood for a moment on the balcony outside of her room,
looking down into the shrubberies, smiled
with pleasure at the splendid mass of color
which lay below her. The rose garden, in
its full blush of summer loveliness, was
splendid with a glory of new-bloomed roses,
whose petals were fast unfolding to the
ardent gaze of their great golden lover, the
sun. It was very early for Gladys to be
about, scarcely seven o'clock, but she had
not slept very well, and so, throwing a loose
wrapper about her, she had stepped out upon
her little balcony and stood looking out on
the fresh beauty of the earth.

For once she was not thinking of herself
or her own beauty, which was, perhaps for
that very reason, the fairest thing in all the
bright picture.

Over across the rose-beds where the flowers nodded a gay good-morning to her, stretched the green lawn, which ran sloping down to the cliffs, at whose foot the waves murmured with a kindly melody.

No other sound was in the land, and in the sea no motion save for the white arms of a youth who was swimming by leisurely, and who slackened his strokes and looked up at the balcony, which showed him a woman who was young and graceful, the distance not allowing him to guess more.

Gladys looked at the swimmer, and thought how graceful were his motions, and how much the boyish head of gold hair and the white, supple, strong limbs, shining through the green waters, added to the scene. It brought human life into what had been before but an empty background; it made her feel that of all the grand things in the world, man may be the grandest. Why did the face of Charles Farwell seem to look at her from the green waves? If it had been

Farwell she could not have seen him, and she knew him to be a thousand miles away. And yet, when the youth out there, lying in the cool water, raised one arm and waved a greeting to her, she answered it involuntarily, and then, remembering for the first moment herself, standing out in the broad daylight in her wrapper, her hair streaming about her shoulders, her little rosy feet bare, she gave a startled cry and sprang back into her room, blushing hotly though no one was there to see.

Her maid came to her in half an hour, bringing the morning mail. She was surprised to see that one of the letters bore the handwriting of her cousin, Amelia Carleton, who was still at Lenox. The first part of the letter she glanced through carelessly, but the last paragraph fixed her attention; she read it slowly, and afterwards sat looking at it abstractedly.

"I hear that your last conquest is the good-looking Englishman we met driving that day. I have asked Lady Carew, who is staying here, all about him. He is the son of Lord Lucre, she tells me ; she knows his family well. It is, as you know, an excellent one in point of position ; and this young man is better off than most younger sons, for he has his mother's whole fortune, which is something very handsome. The elder brother has epilepsy, will never marry, and your friend is sure sooner or later to succeed to the title and estates. Lady Carew says it will probably be sooner, for his brother is not expected to live long. Now, if things have gone as far as I suppose they have, my solemn advice to you, Gladys, is to marry Mr. Larkington. He is the sort of man best calculated to make you happy, as he brings all the things you need most, — money, an assured position, and in time a title. My dear, take the advice of a lonely woman, an old maid, and do not hesitate. You have grown, as I did before you, too *difficile.* It is the curse of American girls with beauty or money, that they have so many chances to marry. They discard this one for one fault, that one because he lacks some certain virtue ; in fine, they end by expecting to find a paragon, which shall unite all the virtues and be without any of the faults of manhood. Of course they don't find him, and they remain unmarried and unhappy. I am opening my heart to you, child, though it hurts me more than you can guess, because I would warn you from the mistake which has made my life cold and empty, my nature hard and the world says selfish. You know I always am ready to keep my promise of giving you the trousseau and the wedding. I should so like to give a house-warming and wedding at once. The house will be ready in a fortnight, when I shall take possession of it."

This letter seemed to change the face of nature to Gladys. She saw no beauty now in sea or sky, the sunshine even seemed to have grown cold, and she began to dress slowly and absently.

She sat down at her toilette glass, placed where the most searching light fell upon it, and, leaning her head upon her hand, proceeded to study with great care the image which the faithful mirror showed her. She looked older, ten years older, than she had done when she stood on the balcony with a smile on her lips. The thought which drew hard lines about her mouth, and marked her

forehead with two strait dints, had come only
with her cousin's letter.   She took her silver
comb (she would have liked a golden one)
and parted the thick soft hair on her left
temple.   Yes, there they were, those first
terrible finger-marks of time.   White hairs —
a few, half a dozen, perhaps — just in this
spot flecked the dusky mass of hair.   No one
knew of their existence but Gladys and her
maid.   The Abigail assured her that they
were the result of some knock she must have
given her head, for only in this spot was
there one to be found; but Gladys refused
to console herself with this hypothesis, and
accepted the warning which they gave her of
the instability of beauty and the flight of
time.

For a quarter of an hour she sat motion-
less, her eyes fixed upon her own shadow,
and in that space she reviewed all her past,
looked her present in the face, and weighed
the possibilities of the future, quietly, coolly,
and methodically.   She put aside the rose-

colored illusions in which women wrap their thoughts of themselves to their very selves, and looked, for once in her life, at the hard plain facts of her existence.

She had passed her first youth, girlhood was behind her, and at twenty-five she was a woman. Her beauty was still at its height, but it must wane, and the waning must begin before long. She had not so many chances open to her of changing her name as she had had last year, and every twelve months the chances would grow less and less. She had that very week walked as a bridesmaid before a bride whose bridegroom, a year previous, had declared himself desolate and broken-hearted at her refusal of his suit. He had consoled himself in so short a time with a pretty chit of eighteen, with pale, pleading blue eyes, and no figure at all! The constancy of man! But there was Cid. Did he still love her? She doubted it. He had never told her so since her return from Europe, though he had had many chances to do so. Then his abrupt departure from Newport without one word of farewell, beyond the *Au revoir* written on the card which came with a bunch of red roses. Did not that imply that he did not wish to see anything more of her? Perhaps he had seen how things would go between herself and Larkington, and wished to prove that he did not consider himself as a *prétendant* for her hand, so left the ground clear for the new suitor. It seemed more than likely. It was rather unkind of Cid, though; but did she deserve anything better from him? She grew quite red as she asked herself the question. And on seeing the flush mount to her forehead in the mirror, she sprang to her feet, angry and defiant, at war with herself, and with a bitter cry against the cruelty of fate, in her heart.

She dressed herself not the less with great care, and chose the dark blue gown in which Larkington had first seen her at the Casino, and which he preferred to any other of her dresses. She was going to the picnic, and had half promised to drive out with the Englishman. She knew, with the unfailing instinct of a woman, that if she drove with him to-day, she would be asked the most serious question which man can put to woman. For a week past he had tried to see her alone, he had sought for an opportunity to speak the words which she was not ready to hear, and she had with a hundred artifices, so skilful that he had not perceived them, put off the decisive moment.

She breakfasted, or made a pretence of so doing, with Mrs. Fallow-Deer in that good lady's boudoir, — a charming little room, hung in sea-green silk, and furnished in veritable antique carved wood.

As Mrs. Fallow-Deer sat in a high-backed chair, pouring tea from a classic urn, a fearful and wonderful pyramid of laces and ribbons placed on the summit of her poll, Gladys looked at her and sighed deeply. This, then, was the end of it all. The kind soul who sat opposite her had been a beauty, too, in her day, but what trace was left of her lost graces! She sighed again, at which unusual sound Mrs. Fallow-Deer put down her teacup and, looking searchingly at Gladys, said slowly and solemnly, —

"My dear, it is my private opinion that you are in love."

Gladys laughed. "I wish I were," she cried half bitterly, half in jest. "Like Patience, I am quite ignorant of the sensation of the tender passion. I have never been in love."

"That is nonsense, my dear; however, it is a nonsense that all girls talk, and I suppose I can't expect you to be wiser than your kind. But seriously, my child, are you not thinking a good deal about somebody?"

"Yes, but that somebody is myself."

"Of course it is always so with a girl who has no business to be a girl any longer. I have had something of your experience, Gladys, and my advice ought not to be valueless to you. I did not marry until I was a year or two older than you, and was heartily sick of myself, and of thinking about myself, and of all the shadowy joys and triumphs I was supposed to enjoy. Now, you have a heart, and were meant to love (as was I) something and somebody besides yourself. Suppose the man whom you marry is not your young ideal; what of that? All men are troublesome comforts, but it 's a great thing to have a companion of your own time, whose interests are one with your own, and who will go with you through life. My dear, it is very dreary to sit over the embers alone. Husbands are at best a good deal of a trial, but then the compensation comes in one's children. I am a woman who has, as you know, experienced a great deal and enjoyed many things, but the comfort and pleasure I have had in my boys outweighs all the rest of the goods of my life beyond comparison. But I suppose you can't understand that."

Gladys had not sat patiently during this homily, but had moved uneasily about the room, looking first out of the window and then into the cream jug on the table, as if to find some help there. Everybody seemed to be against her and in league with Larkington, for she knew perfectly well to what all Mrs. Fallow-Deer had said pointed. Even Charlie, — his absence from Newport was in itself a sanction to her encouragement of Larkington.

A servant entered, bringing a great bunch of deep gold yellow roses for Miss Carleton, and a note in an already familiar hand. It was from Larkington, asking her if she would drive with him to the picnic. She stood still and silent for one awful moment, during which it seemed to her that the whole of her life hung in the balance. Should she go, or not? She sat down at the writing-desk, took up a quill, examined its point carefully, took out a sheet of paper, dated it, wrote, "Dear Mr. Larkington," and had not yet decided whether the next phrase should be one of refusal or acceptance.

The letter meant so much more than a mere invitation to drive; if she accepted it, she knew the results. Could she? The forbidding face of Amelia Carleton, once as handsome and attractive as her own, rose before her, hard, unyielding, frozen, and expressionless! "I will go with pleasure," were the words she wrote, and, signing herself as "Cordially yours," she despatched the note, and then, going to the glass, spent the next ten minutes in fastening the breast-knot of roses which Larkington had sent her, over her slow-beating heart.

The pin with which she fastened the roses she noticed was one of Herr Goldzchink's minor presents, which, when the others had been sent back to her discarded German lover, had been overlooked, and had only been discovered the week before in a drawer of her jewel-case.

On the hand which held the roses to her

breast was one small old ring.   It was of
very little value, and had cost Charles Farwell the first score of dollars he had earned,
all those years ago.   She smiled a little sadly
as she looked at the ring, and then kissed it
and slipped it off from her finger.

CHAPTER VIII.

MR. LARKINGTON stood looking anxiously from his window, on the morning of the all-important day of Mr. Gray Grosvenor's picnic. That gentleman himself, passing by and catching a glimpse of Larkington's rather gloomy face, nodded reassuringly to him, as if to say that the little cloud which had just floated before the face of the sun did not mean anything. The weather would not think of doing so ill-judged a thing as to interfere with one of Mr. Gray Grosvenor's fêtes. So on passed the great man, wrapped in a mysterious vision of the new mode of cooking macaroni with madeira sauce, and the effect it would have upon the experienced palates of Mr. Belhomme and Mrs. Fallow-Deer.

Larkington's anxiety had no reference to the weather, or to the prospects of the picnic, but was centred in the small and dainty billet which his quick eye already detected in the hand of Stirrups, who appeared on the horizon, bearing down for the hotel.

Stirrups, a hideous little gnome of a groom, was dressed in a neat and precise livery, and walked gravely and composedly up to the side entrance of the hotel, giving a glance at the small window in the third story where he had rightly expected to see Larkington's face.

He passed through the hall and up the first flight of stairs with the slow and condescending step which these gentlemen of the rumble affect when they are obliged to touch the vulgar earth with their feet, being used to be carried by the swiftest steeds and driven by the fairest of ladies. In the upper corridor he saw no one, nor on the stairs above or below, and at once, losing the grand air and his slow step, he ran up the next two flights, taking three steps at a time, and rushed, without knocking, into his master's apartment. Breathless he thrust the letter into his hand, and stood panting, his eyes fixed on Larkington's face.

The master, without noticing the unceremonious entrance of the man, tore open the note, glanced at its contents, and, flushing with what he read, cried aloud, —

" It 's all right, Stirrups! By Jove ! I was nervous, though. What the —— kept you such a time ? " Without waiting for an answer, Larkington continued: " Now we have n't more than time. I must be there at twelve o'clock. Bring the trap up and look sharp. Remember you are to be missing when the break-up comes. I shall stay till the last."

Stirrups did "look sharp," and at twelve o'clock precisely the wheels of Mr. Larkington's dogcart crunched along the gravel driveway which led to Mrs. Fallow-Deer's house. Gladys heard the sound and it made her shiver.

" ' Hear it not, Duncan ; for it is a knell
That summons thee to heaven or to ——.'

Not a very pretty place to talk about," she cried, as she rose slowly from her seat in Mrs. Fallow-Deer's morning-room.

" What an odd girl you are, Gladys ! Well, good-by. I shall be out, tell Gray Grosvenor, by half-past one. Make him wait luncheon till I come. Don't forget your dish of croquettes, nor the champagne; they are all packed in a basket in the hall. Are you warmly enough dressed, child? How pale you look ! Give your cheeks a little rub, so ! That 's better. Now trot along, and remember what I said to you at breakfast."

Gladys did look pale, and listless too, as she stepped into the dogcart, steadied by Mr. Larkington's hand; but he thought she never before had looked so lovely. There was a shadow in the eyes, which were usually so open and clear, without dissimulation or consciousness.

Larkington was not quite himself either,

and the two people, who usually chatted like magpies on the hundred light topics which are the straws on which society conversations are kept afloat, hardly spoke during the drive to the picnic ground.

Stirrups, sitting behind with folded arms and stony face, seemed to feel the constraint of his betters, which he himself shared.

At the entrance of the Glen, the spot chosen for the picnic, they encountered Mr. Gray Grosvenor, who welcomed them cordially but hurriedly. He was one of those hosts who cannot give themselves time to welcome quietly the guests who have arrived, but whose eyes and thoughts are forever wandering to the next comers, who may be of more importance than the ones whom he is at that moment greeting.

"Ah, how de doo, Miss Gladys? Ah, um, um, Larkington, delighted to see you. Basket? oh yes, um, yes, thanks, yes; give it to the waiter. Good of you, I 'm sure. Yes, yes, you 'll find my sister in the Glen.

Wait for Mrs. Fallow-Deer? oh, um, yes, yes, of course, of course." And he turned to speak to some later arrivals.

Larkington drove down the picturesque road which hangs over a miniature precipice, with a miniature stream at the bottom, and a large mill and mill-wheel, " as romantic in its appearance as the one used in Sonnambula at Her Majesty's," so Larkington said.

The road leads into a wide, open space, with enough shade trees to insure coolness, but without a trace of dampness. Long tables were spread beneath the tall oaks, and dainties of every kind loaded the boards.

The little brook ran babbling merrily by on one side, but its melody was quickly drowned in the loud strains of an orchestra, hidden by a group of thick palm-trees, brought out from town for the occasion. A dancing pavilion with a smooth floor had been built up during the previous day and night, and was gayly decorated with flags, Japanese lanterns, fans, and umbrellas.

The Glen was in holiday dress, tricked out with every art of the decorator and florist. The lovely green turf, with its sprinkling of fragrant pine-needles, might not touch the silken-clad feet of the ladies, though, and rich rugs were spread about to keep the delicate shoes from contact with mother earth's fairest carpet. The very stems of the dignified oak-trees were garlanded with colored streamers. They looked abashed at all these trappings, the poor country trees, and rustled uncomfortably at the incongruity of their appearance.

Two great elm-trees stand side by side at the lower part of the Glen, fair enough to be the scene of the revels of the fairy queen, and between their straight trunks one can look out and see the river, or arm of the sea, which washes the pebbly shore. But the simplicity of the view and its quiet beauty had evidently annoyed the perverted taste of Mr. Gray Grosvenor or his assistants, and an arch of sunflowers spanned the distance which intervened between the two great trees, so that even that view was spoiled to the few among the company who knew and loved the Glen in its wild and natural beauty.

Among those few persons who were not so loud in praises of the "beautiful decorations" as the rest of the company were Mrs. Craig and Count Clawski! How they came there, what power had been brought to bear on Gray Grosvenor to induce him at the eleventh hour to revoke his decision to leave out the pretty little Baltimorean, Gladys was not able to discover. But there she was, all smiles and roses and dimples, as pretty a creature in her rainbow draperies as was to be seen on that bright summer morning.

The Count, who was something of an artist, was really a good deal disturbed by the sunflowers and Japanese decorative knick-knacks, which he affirmed would spoil his appetite.

Mrs. Craig, who in heart had loved the

whole *Jardin Mabille* appearance of the place,
quickly took the cue from him, and said,
sotto voce, to Gladys, —

" Shocking bad taste; don't you think so,
dear ? "

" I had not thought about it," said Gladys,
frankly. " There is perhaps a little too much
of it, but you know I am rather barbaric in
my taste and like all sorts of gay-colored
things."

The majority of the guests were of Gladys's
opinion, and on the arrival of Mrs. Fallow-
Deer the whole company — some sixty souls
— sat down to meat in high spirits and with
excellent appetites. Meat, did I say? Ay,
and to fish of every sort, and game, — all that
there was in or out of season, — shell fish,
too, from the beatific little neck clam to the
rubicund lobster, pâtés and game pies, galan-
tines and roast fowls, Mayonnaises, Lyon-
naises, *fry'on'aiseys*, mushrooms, jellies, ices,
blanc-manges, fruits, cakes, wines, cordials,
and finally, by way of a saving grace, coffee.

"I notice that the Americans have the largest appetites and the worst digestions of any people in the world," said Count Clawski to his left-hand neighbor, Gladys Carleton.

The Count's appetite was missing on this festive occasion, and it was owing to this fact that he spoke so bitterly, and thought so bitterly too, of the dinner last night at Mrs. Craig's, where he had overeaten himself. However, his ill temper was too small a drop of gall in the cup of jollity of the company to have any noticeable effect, and the luncheon went off as gayly as possible.

Mr. Belhomme and Mr. Gray Grosvenor toasted each other, and were more friendly than they had been since their memorable dispute over the best method of serving chicken livers, which had interrupted for two years a friendship of a lifetime. Society agreed that it was better that they did make the matter up, for it would be difficult to decide which of the two *gourmets* was the better authority on chicken livers, as they both had every reason to consider themselves *connois-seurs* in this particular dish.

Mrs. Fallow-Deer tasted of nearly every dish, and grew rosier and jollier at every course.

Of all the guests there gathered, two only seemed a little out of the general tone of mirth and jollity, and these two were the very ones in whom we have the most interest. Gladys Carleton was inclined to be quiet and *distraite*, eating little, and that little with nervous haste. Larkington's appetite was not so voracious as it might have been, considering the fact that for the last week he had breakfasted on a roll from the bake-shop brought in surreptitiously by Stirrups, and a cup of tea made over the gas-burner by that same devoted individual, who, as financial affairs grew darker for his master, became more and more familiar with him, and comforted by a touching devotion the man to whom he was loyally attached.

The very rolls for the morning's scanty

meal were bought with the gratuities which
Stirrups had received from various of his
master's friends, in compensation for some
slight services.   The cigar which Larkington
had smoked on the morning of the picnic
had been given to Stirrups by Mr. Belhomme,
a week before, when he had taken a stone
from the hoof of that gentleman's horse.
The groom, foreseeing the not unprecedented
state of affairs which was approaching, had
put by the fragrant Havana, and on the
morning of the memorable picnic had laid
it beside Larkington's plate at his frugal
breakfast.

If the master did not make a good luncheon, the man, with glistening eyes, surveyed
the luxuriously spread tables, and chose the
various dishes which he would attack vigor-
ously, when the time should come for him
and his fellows to gather up the fragments
of the feast.

At last — it seemed to the hungry Stirrups a very long luncheon — Mr. Gray Gros-

venor rose from his chair, and the worshipful company of the elect had finished their mid-day repast, whose chief and greatest charm had been that it had been eaten beneath the canopy of God's blue sky, between the walls of living green, and in the pure air, sweet with the stacks of new-mown grass and clover in the field hard by.

The sunflowers in stiff florist's garlands, the colored paper gewgaws, were, to an over-sensitive mind, a discord; but few among the guests detected the inharmoniousness of trimming, with art intended to be decorative, one of the most beautiful bits of nature in the idyllic island. And there was not one among them who was not made the better, the more kindly, by that day passed among the ferns and sweet-briers of Glen Anna.

The dance in the pavilion was rather a failure. Somehow, the incongruity of the little stiff town bouquets and the flimsy favors seemed to strike most of the company, and the cotillon only included the army

of veteran waltzers, grown old in the practice
of their favorite step, of whom Gray Grosvenor was the major-general.

The young people wandered off in groups,
some of them climbing the hill to get a
wider view. Others explored the damp and
mildewed granaries of the old mill, while
all to whom the seaboard was native were
drawn to the beach, where the wavelets gently
lapped the stony shore.

At the back of the narrow beach rises a
bank on which some charitable person has
placed a bench beneath the shadow of a
group of heavy shade trees. On this bench
Gladys and Larkington seated themselves,
and the girl, collecting a heap of flat pebbles
at her feet, tried to skip them across the
water.

Larkington watched her as she rose and
stood, intent on making her pebbles skip
three times; she was so willowy and graceful, standing just beside him, touching him
with her dress, quite within his reach, that

he longed to stretch out his arms and clasp
the round waist, the graceful shoulders, the
charms which every line of the dark blue
dress outlined or concealed.

It would be so much easier, so much more
natural, to ask her then the question which
he knew he must that day ask her, when she
could guess, from the beating of his heart,
the meaning of the words which might come
incoherently; if he could but once touch her
lips with his own, the frosty spell that held
him silent would be broken and he could
give words to the feelings which troubled
him. If he only dared — they were alone —
why not? Why should he not woo her as he
had the flaxen-haired German girl who now
loved him as she had ever since the day
when they had first kissed in the shadow
of the Black Forest. Poor Frieda! why
should he remember her, so long since deserted, on this splendid day, when he sat at
the feet of another woman whom he loved
with the full force of his being?

The chill of the reminiscence, the cool look in the eyes of Gladys Carleton as she stooped to pick up another pebble, arrested his arms stretched impulsively toward her. He altered his attitude rather clumsily, and sprang to his feet as if the gesture which she had seen had been only an effort to steady himself in rising.

But Gladys had both seen and understood it, and after making a last and most successful toss of her biggest stone, she said, —

" I think we had better go back now; don't you ? "

As they rejoined the party, the band was striking up the music for a Virginia reel. The long lines were formed upon the greensward, and were headed by Mrs. Fallow-Deer and Mr. Gray Grosvenor.

" Stand at the foot, Miss Gladys and Larkington ! " cried the light-footed and lighter-witted host. " Now then, off we go !"

And off they did go at a great pace, Mrs. Fallow-Deer dancing to Larkington, and Mr.

Gray Grosvenor bowing to Gladys. Down
the long row of dancers that intervened between the head and the foot, tripped the
young-hearted matron and bobbed a courtesy,
back again, and down once more to turn,
giving the right hand, then to favor Larkington with the left. Then both pudgy hands
were offered to the long-limbed Englishman,
who could shake a foot in the reel with the
best of them. Her rotund back contrasted
with his sinewy outline in the *dos-à-dos*, and
then began the turning of the gentlemen.
First came the breathless dowager to Count
Clawski, who with a grave court bow turned
her slowly and sedately about, and returned
her to Gray Grosvenor, waiting for his partner
after having squeezed the pretty hand of Mrs.
Craig until her ring cut her finger. Mr.
Belhomme next hopped briskly about her
portly form, doing all the turning himself,
and again she returned to the charge of
Gray Grosvenor, who, after another turn,
relinquished her to her son, a graceless

youth, who clasped his mother's waist and whirled her off her feet. At last after many adventures she reached the foot, exhausted but cheerful, and the next couple had their turn.

It was a grand dance, everybody said when it was over, and Mrs. Fallow-Deer received many congratulations on her brisk dancing.

Larkington's spirits had been raised to a very high point by the dance, and a parting bottle of champagne cracked with Count Clawski failed to lower them. When the time came for him to lift Gladys into the dogcart, he felt equal to any feat of prowess, even that of asking this tall proud girl if she would be his wife, and accept the endowment of all his worldly goods, which at that moment might easily have been packed in his large portmanteau, in exchange for the millions which he supposed to be her dower.

Gladys, too, seemed less like a statue than she had been half an hour before by the sea-shore. Her pale cheeks were a little flushed from the long fatiguing reel, her dark heavy hair had become somewhat loosened, and one perfumed mesh had escaped from the comb which fastened it.

As Larkington helped her into the carriage, the wind blew the soft tress against his lips; it felt like a caress, and he sprang after her, taking the reins from the strange groom who held them.

" I have lost my man; it's a most extraordinary thing; he is usually the most steady, punctual creature. I am afraid that Mr. Gray Grosvenor treated the coachmen too well, and that Stirrups did not show himself because he knew it would be better for him not to be seen," said Larkington.

" I suppose you can manage the horses for once without the moral support of your groom, and, as a consoling thought, remember that I am an excellent whip."

" If you can manage horses half as well as you manage men, Miss Gladys, I would back your driving against the field."

"I suppose you mean that for a compliment, Mr. Larkington, but, upon my word, I do not consider it such. I have never before been told that 'managing' was one of my characteristics."

"I did not mean that; you are perverse, but it does not matter. You look just as lovely when you play at being cross as when you are smiling. I wish you would always wear that wreath of oak leaves on your hat; it makes you look so much more like the girls at home, and so much less of a great lady."

Gladys did not quite understand this speech. How could she fancy that Larkington, moved by a real feeling, had half forgotten himself, and told her frankly what was in his mind? At the nutting parties in the village where he had grown up, the girls used all to wear these pretty chaplets on their uncovered heads, when they came home together, their tin pails filled with fruit, their hands stained with the juices of the nuts.

A look of surprise in the girl's face showed

him what he had said, and, remembering the business he had in hand, he determined to plunge *in medias res*, and so, gathering all his forces together, he said with a voice that was not quite natural, —

"Of course you must have seen how much I am in love with you, Gladys, and I cannot stand the uncertainty any longer; will you marry me?"

Gladys thought, of all the proposals she had ever listened to, — they had been in number exactly twenty-five, an average of one a year for her whole life, — this one certainly was the most abrupt. But she had been prepared for it, and with a sense of thankfulness for the form in which the fatal question had been asked, she said quietly, her eyes fixed on the rumble of Mrs. Fallow-Deer's carriage in front of them, —

"Yes, I will."

For he had not asked her if she loved him, and she had been spared the lie, which her proud lips could hardly have spoken.

CHAPTER IX.

It was exactly half-past five o'clock on Saturday afternoon when Gladys Carleton pronounced those three words which made Larkington for the moment consider himself the most triumphant man in the wide world.

At exactly half-past five o'clock on the same Saturday afternoon, Charles Farwell said to Mr. John Cartwright, his only companion, —

" Jack, I must start for home to-night."

" You 're not in earnest, Charlie ? "

" Yes, old man, in dead earnest."

" What has made you change your mind so suddenly ? "

Charles Farwell was silent, and Cartwright stood leaning against the damp wall of the mine. The only light that showed the two men's faces to each other came from the candles in their miner's hats. The feeble rays lighted up a small space of the gallery of the silver mine where they were standing, and beyond, on either side, all was black and dark.

It was not easy to recognize the exquisitely dressed New Yorker whom we left at Newport, in the man sitting on a mound of earth, dressed in a red shirt, corduroy breeches, and top boots, all besplashed and bemired with the dark mud of the mine. He looked infinitely more original and individual in this dress, which showed his fine well-knit body and strong limbs. His hair, untroubled for the past six weeks by barber's shears, had grown rather longer than Gladys Carleton had seen it since his childhood, and the curl had got the better of him, as it had in those old days.

Jack Cartwright stood looking at his friend with a puzzled expression. Farwell had come to Leadville in answer to his telegram telling him of the new vein which he had found in the mine which was their joint property, and had remained ever since, working with him, and making plans for the best running of the mine, which Cartwright was sure would make their fortunes.

They had been college chums, and the friendship begun so early in life was a very strong one. Cartwright had led a rolling-stone existence during the ten years that had elapsed since he had left college, and had certainly gathered no moss.

Farwell, on the contrary, had led a quiet, industrious life, working hard in a broker's office in Wall Street, and making a comfortable income for himself, with which he managed to do just twice as many charitable acts as did his employer, a man whose fortune was estimated by millions.

Just about a year before the date of the despatch which had called Farwell to Leadville so suddenly, Jack Cartwright had come to him absolutely without means of subsistence, but full of visions of a great fortune he could realize if Farwell would supply him with the capital to buy a certain Leadville claim which Cartwright was persuaded would prove to be a mine of riches. The man who owned the claim was not of the same sanguine mind, and so Cartwright got it for a mere song, Farwell paying the piper. With varying small successes Cartwright had worked the claim until the discovery of the rich vein of ore. Farwell had, since his arrival, summoned the aid of several mining experts, and had finally satisfied himself of the real value of the property, which he had always considered worthless, as did every one else except the hopeful Cartwright. Once sure of the solid value of the mine, the next requisite step was the forming of a company to work it, and it had been decided that Cartwright should go to New York, and make all the necessary arrangements for the starting of such a company, while Farwell remained in charge of the "claim."

The two friends had been making a tour of inspection through the deserted galleries of the mine, which were so soon to be filled with a crowd of toiling miners, when Farwell suddenly announced his intention of returning to the East.

Receiving no answer to his last question, Cartwright asked again somewhat more emphatically, —

" What the deuce has put such an idea into your head, Charlie ? "

" You did not hear any sound, I suppose, a minute ago ? " said Farwell.

" No. What was it like ? "

" It was the sound of a woman's voice, and it called my name. No, Cartwright, I did not suppose that you had heard the voice ; but I did. It was the voice of the woman I love ; she called to me in distress. I must go to her."

He rose as he spoke, looked into the darkness dreamily, and then walked with a quick, determined pace down the gallery, Cartwright

following him, more and more amazed by the
words of his friend. It was not like Farwell, this sort of thing; he could not understand it, and, thinking the close air of the
mine might have affected his head, he took
his friend by the arm, and they soon were
out of the dark, damp, underground region,
where thousands of human beings are con-
demned to pass the greater part of their lives
in toiling for treasures for other men to
waste, out into the pure air of the splendid
September day.

Their eyes, accustomed to the darkness of
the mine, were dazzled by the light, and Farwell shaded the too sudden glory of the sunshine with his hand. In the vast open plain
where they found themselves were many
works, some of them deserted and dilapi-
dated, others with every sign of busy mining life about them. The rude buildings
which stood at the mouth of their mine
were fallen into a lamentable state of unre-
pair, but to the sanguine eyes of Cartwright

they were already repaired and in good condition.

In the little office, the one room which boasted a whole roof, were collected all Cartwright's worldly possessions, and into this apartment he led the way. Farwell stood leaning against the door-post, his eyes fixed on the wonderful scene spread before him. Across the wide plain, two miles distant, lay the city of Leadville, a straggling town, at this distance picturesque, outlined against the high mountains which lie beyond it, rough, inaccessible, and grand. The clearness of the atmosphere in this country is most deceptive, and the sun-tipped range of hills seemed within easy walking distance. The summits, which earlier in the day had been dazzling white, were now touched into a soft rosy color by the warm reflection of the sunset tints, and the sky had softened to a dim and tender blue, more restful to the eyes than the intense and vivid color of mid-day.

"Well, Charlie, we must be off if you are

in earnest about starting to-night," said Cart-wright, as he unhitched the bridle of his mus-tang. Farwell nodded an assent, and mounting their horses the two friends rode off across the arid plain, whose soil produces nothing but a few scraggy fir-trees, and the short grayish grass so common in mining districts.

As Farwell rode through Chestnut Street, he said with a half-sigh, —

"Jack, I am sorry to go, for some reasons. I have not been here long enough to feel the monotony which must come, I suppose, and I still am bound by the novelty and freshness of the existence here. There is a vigor and youth about the country which we in the East have lost already; before we have grown to our prime, we are old."

"Yes," said Jack; "remember this is the boss mining camp of the world that you are turning your back upon, because of an echo in the mine that you fancy is the voice of some woman. It 's not like you, Charlie, to be so deuced fanciful."

"Is n't it? Well, I don't know. I may come back, Jack, and become a pioneer of the new State, a leading man in Colorado; but I doubt it. If the voice did not call me, if she tells me she did not want to see me, then I shall be back as soon as the business can be settled. But if it was the voice of Gladys Carleton, you will have to manage the mine by yourself, and I will take care of the city interests. I suppose you and I will be called rich men in a month's time, Jack?"

"Yes, I suppose we will, if you don't get muddled by hearing any more of these echoes," said Cartwright, peevishly. "I don't feel altogether satisfied to have the matter in your hands; are you sure your head 's all right?"

Farwell laughed, and answered more briskly than he had done since he had heard the echo in the mine. Seeing that his friend was really concerned about his wits, he proceeded to discuss the prospects and the business arrangements they had decided upon in his usual clear manner.

Before the two men parted that night, Cartwright was quite satisfied that it was for the best that he should remain, and his partner make the necessary journey to New York.

CHAPTER X.

THE journey from Leadville to Cheyenne is not without interest, nor did it so prove to Charles Farwell. To all intelligent travellers there is much to be learned in the course of a long journey, both from observation of the country through which they pass, and in conversation with their fellow-travellers.

At Cheyenne, the point where the great transcontinental railroad crosses the local line of travel, Farwell arrived early one September morning. Awaiting the advent of the Eastward-bound train forty or fifty men were assembled at the small wooden station-house. Every variety of costume was worn, from the conventional suit of American morning dress to the picturesque garb of the Mongolian. Long-haired, red-shirted herders conversed familiarly with gentlemen whose clothes might have been forwarded them to this remote spot by Poole. A Mexican *ranchero* with a wide *sombrero* and high boots paced up and down the narrow plank platform, talking earnestly with a smart-looking man of the Teutonic race.

From the scraps of their conversation, Farwell gathered that the Mexican was consulting the German professionally, on the subject of his wife's health. Farwell learned from a loquacious Jew, a commercial traveller who entered into conversation with him, that the Mexican lived fifty miles distant, and had ridden over to procure medicine for his ailing wife from the medical practitioner of Cheyenne. The same obliging personage gave Farwell brief sketches of the most prominent of the individuals who stood about the platform, leaning against the station or sitting on the steps.

" That little fellow there with the red beard is an Englishman ; calls himself at home Lord

Archie Alvesworth, at Cheyenne he drops
the title. He owns a great cattle ranch, ten
miles from here, which he manages himself.
He has lots of friends visiting him, and they
have a pretty gay time of it at his shanty."

"Who is the old man with the long white
hair?" asked Farwell, pointing to a tall
figure wrapped in a long loose gray cloak.

"That is the Frenchman. He is rather
light in the upper story. That young girl
upon whose arm he is leaning is his daughter. I can't tell you their real names; they
have only been here a few months, and they
are a queer, silent lot. The old fellow fan-
cies he has found a diamond mine, and he
and the daughter, with an old servant they
brought with them, are always searching and
digging for the wonderful mine that will
make their fortune."

The face of the Frenchman was that of an
enthusiast. The white hair and furrowed
brow were all the signs of age which he
showed. The bright eyes, alert step, and

the expectant expression of the face indi-
cated a sanguine and volatile nature. The
girl who walked by his side had nothing remarkable in her appearance, save in the
pathos of her eyes, which haunted Farwell
for months after.

Inside the comfortless wooden building
was a long bare room which served for a
restaurant. Here all was bustle and hurry.
The keeper of the establishment was over-
looking half a dozen men, who were arrang-
ing the tables. His wife, a lank, raw-boned
New Englander, was making thick sand-
wiches with heavy saleratus bread and large
wedges of ham, cut from a still smoking
joint. In an adjoining apartment the two
bar-tenders, in the lightest possible costumes,
were busy mixing drinks for the thirsty mul-
titude of loungers. The grated ice rang
musically in the tumblers, and the sound of
the julep was pleasant to the ears of those
who were anticipating a refreshing draught,
while it recalled to those who had already

partaken, the agreeable sensation of the cool liquid trembling down the parched throat.

It was terribly hot. Even the dogs seemed to suffer, for they crouched within the shadow of the long building. The men bore the extreme heat with resignation; they spoke on every subject of conversation save the weather, — as if by common consent this topic was avoided.

A smart covered wagon drawn by a pair of strong mules rattled up to the station. From the vehicle a man descended, carrying a child of two years of age in his arms. He placed the little creature on the platform, and turned to assist its mother from the wagon. She was a healthy, strapping young woman, dressed in a neat silk gown, and wearing a bonnet which must have come from New York. The husband made fast his mules, and the couple entered the express office, where they were hospitably received by the agent.

"That man is Dick Parsons, the stage-

driver. His wife is going to Maine to stop
with her folks. He came down to put her
on board the train."

Farwell's informant, as they passed the
door of the bar-room, made a slight pause,
as if more from habit than from any thought
of entering the room. Farwell, who had
been too much absorbed in watching the
motley crowd of people, and listening to
the brief but comprehensive accounts of
them given by his new friend, to remember
the etiquette of the country, took the gentle
hint, and invited his new acquaintance "to
take something." The invitation was accepted, and the two men entered the bar-
room.

The commercial traveller and the bar-
tender exchanged a wink as the stranger
ordered for himself a plain lemonade. The
Ganymede of Cheyenne station was rather
a sinister-looking fellow, with one eye. His
right hand boasted a thumb and two fingers
only, but the airy skill with which he tossed

the icy fluid from the tin tumbler to the glass one showed that this physical defect did not unfit him for his profession.

As the commercial traveller drained the last drop of his whiskey cocktail, a faint rumbling was heard along the rails, and a few moments after the Eastward train came in sight. Every car window had an earnest face behind it, and the platforms were crowded with the passengers, who hardly waited the stopping of the train, to dash into the restaurant, where the preparations for dinner were now completed. Farwell entered the room with the crowd, and watched the already familiar sight of the hungry beings vainly endeavoring to satisfy themselves with the indifferent food provided for them.

There is bad management somewhere. Whose fault is it? The prices charged by the railroads are so high, that the traveller has a right to demand comfortable meals at a just cost. The patience of the American

people is phenomenal. They are plundered
by railroad corporations who neglect their
comfort, and whose parsimony often endan-
gers their lives; and they bear this patiently,
not even, save on rare occasions, making
the public complaints which are to be found
against like abuses in every issue of the
" London Daily News."

" It is a great virtue, — patience," sighed
Farwell, as he left the table where his healthy
appetite had been somewhat appeased by a
plate of cold pork and beans and a bottle
of warm beer. His cigarette consoled him
.for his bad dinner, and he paced up and
down, looking at the various people from
Cheyenne and its vicinity who, in his two
hours' waiting at the station, had so greatly
interested him. The young French girl had
made friends with one of the passengers, a
mother who had four children tagging about
her. She was carrying the youngest of
these, while the woman and her other children walked up and down, stretching their

cramped limbs. The English lord was talking to the engineer of the train, — an intelligent Scot; and the stage-driver was introducing his pretty wife to the Pullman-car conductor, an important personage in the society of the Pacific Railroad.

This half-hour's chat with the officials on the train, and those among the passengers who are desirous of deriving information or willing to impart the latest news from either coast, is one of the most important events in the day to many of the dwellers by the iron roadway. This link betwixt them and the civilization in which there was no room for. them lessens immeasurably their sense of isolation.

But now the whistle of the engine warned the travellers that the time had come when they must again take up the thread of their journey.

Farwell bade farewell to the commercial gentleman, thanking him for his information. He stepped upon the back platform of the rear car, and looked his last upon the little desolate station and its crowd of *habitués*.

The old French gentleman was already climbing into a rickety vehicle, while his daughter unfastened the hitching-rein. The stage-driver was waving a last adieu to his wife and his little child, wailing at the grief of a first parting. Inside the restaurant its proprietor was seen locking a cash-box which had been filled at the cost of the pockets and digestion of the travellers. The one-eyed bar-tender was the only member of the group of people who was still busy, and his skilled fingers tossed a red liquid from the tin to the crystal tumbler accurately. His task was never done, day or night.

On sped the train, and in a brief space Cheyenne station was lost to view.

As the day waned, the intense heat moderated, and the passengers on the Eastward train revived a little from the wilted condition they had experienced. They could look out now over the wide plains of sunburnt prairie, whose lines were broken at rare intervals by the farm of some courageous settler. Near one of these green oases the train stopped for some trifling repair. Farwell, standing upon the platform, looked with interest at the well-built adobe house and outbuildings, the green trees, and the well-planted garden. The group of cattle, the dogs, and feathered creatures of the barnyard were the only friends whose company the family of this settler could claim. The grounds were enclosed by a curious fence of woven twigs; wood and stone are materials little used on these frontier farms, owing to the great difficulty and expense of transporting them.

What heroism is shown by these men and women, who taking each other by the hand turn from the luxuries of the Eastern civilization and go out to conquer the savage luxuriance of the West! Courage, patience, self-reliance, must he possess who would succeed in this struggle for wealth in the Western wilderness.

As night drew near, trains of emigrants were passed, three or four wagons usually travelling together, for mutual protection. The great white-hooded vehicles, drawn by heavy cattle, moved slowly along. The family, with all their household goods, are packed away in the wagon, which is almost invariably attended by a pair of dogs and several cows. It is a weary road which they must travel over. Long lines of nodding sunflowers at intervals mark out the path of the overland trail.

To Farwell their golden beauty was an intense pleasure ; he asked a fellow-traveller how they came to be so regularly planted, and learned a curious fact from the man whom he had questioned.

In the early days when Brigham Young and his fellow-prophets led out the band of saints to the New Jerusalem of Salt Lake City, across the wide prairies, many hardships were endured. In that first almost heroic journey the emigrants suffered se-

verely from the want of fuel. Young, on his
return to the East, provided himself with
enormous quantities of the seeds of the sun-
flower, which the second band of emigrants
sowed by the way, for the benefit of the
next party of deluded fanatics who should
be enticed from their homes by the wily
prophet. The path over which the Mormons
passed is marked by a golden line, and the
camp-fires of the emigrants to-day are lighted
by the fibrous stalks of the sunflowers which
the Mormon saints sowed forty years ago.

When they reached the station where
supper was awaiting the travellers, Farwell
decided not to venture a second time that
day into a railway restaurant. From his
capacious lunch-basket he drew rations of
crackers and cheese, with a bottle of claret.
His never-failing comfort, the cigarette, was
the only light save that of the stars, as he sat
in his favorite place on the rear platform.

As the train sped on once more through
the night, Farwell sat thinking of Newport,

and all that might have happened there since his departure. He wondered if Gladys had missed him, and then he smiled at the thought. He knew that she must have grieved over his departure. He knew that she loved him now; he had never doubted it since that night when they rode home together through the sweet country lanes of Newport, the very evening before his departure. Then he thought again, and with a sudden pain, of her voice as he had heard it calling him, heavy with distress, full of passionate entreaty. What could it have meant? If any ill had befallen her, he certainly would have learned it by telegraph. He was coming to her now with all the speed of steam and iron, yet the journey seemed so long!

The dark prairie was all about him, — before, behind, on either side, — and the train sped on rapidly. Suddenly, far off, a spark of light broke the blackness of the night. It grew brighter and clearer, as the train approached it, and he now saw that it came from a fire. Not a chance flame lit by a wayward spark, but a neatly built camp-fire, cheerful and comfortable. The flames crackled about a gypsy kettle, and shone on a great white wagon standing tenantless by the wayside. The tired oxen were lying near by, their noses hidden by their bags of fodder. A group of people sat at a short distance from the blaze, just where their figures were lighted by the flame. A woman seated on the ground, an infant in her arms, looking up into the face of the man who stood behind her, erect, and in the uncertain light seeming to be of a heroic build. These three, all alone in the midst of the vast prairie, with hope for their guide, and love for their companion. This was a home, though the next evening would see the trio far on their journey, and the kettle would swing over a fire some twenty miles nearer its final destination.

For one moment was the life picture before Farwell, warm, happy, full of a deep significance, and then the train carried him past it away into the night. The cheerful blaze grew dim again in the distance, and finally was lost in the darkness. The remembrance of that camp-fire, and the group seen by its light, remained with Charles Farwell when many friends had been forgotten, in the lapse of time.

At last the journey was accomplished, and though it had been full of color and interest, it was with a feeling of intense relief that Charles Farwell stepped from the train at Jersey City. Five minutes later, our traveller found himself on the ferry-boat which conveys the passengers from the railroad terminus in Jersey to the metropolis of New York.

It was late in the afternoon, and Farwell, standing in the open part of the boat, looked out over the busy scene which spread itself on either hand. The tangle of the shipping spread across the heaven like an enormous cobweb. The cool, green waters of the bay were churned into a hundred streaks of white foam by the furrowing paddle-wheels of the ferry-boats which ply to and fro between the great centre and its outlying dependencies. The boats themselves were laden with such dense crowds of human beings that it seemed impossible to fancy that there were any men and women left in the city.

On reaching the landing, Farwell, giving his checks to the minion of the express, mounted the stairs of the Elevated Railroad. He entered the train, and in a breathless haste was whirled up town by that wonderful line of travel which hangs, like the coffin of Mahomet, 'twixt earth and heaven. It had never struck him before that the Elevated Railroad was a particularly noticeable feature of New York. After his sojourn in Colorado, every detail which goes to make the vast convenience of the city of Manhattan impressed him.

" We are too civilized," sighed our traveller, as he stepped from the train at the Twenty-third Street Station. As he walked down the long flight of stairs, he smiled at the thought which passed through his mind. He had invented a plan for transporting the passengers of the Elevated Railroad up and down the long stairs which lead to the stations by means of a slide, in the very moment when he had protested against the ultra convenience of the Elevated Road.

At Delmonico's the great dining-room was crowded with the same set of people he had left dining there on the night when he had started for Leadville. After Farwell had ordered his dinner with a certain care, — it was many weeks since he had *dined*, — he leaned back in his chair and looked about the brilliantly lighted apartments.

At the table on his right sat Hewson, the coolest speculator in Wall Street. His shadow, Hangon, a man triple his size, had just given his directions to the servant for dinner. The speculator looked careworn, his thin face was flushed, and his hand shook as he raised his glass to his lips. The client Hangon addressed some remark to the great man, who answered him shortly and rudely. The face of the mighty parasite flushed at the rebuff, but his vexation was cooled and soothed in the beaker of wine which he drained at the expense of his patron.

Presently Hewson spoke, rapidly and earnestly. Farwell could not hear the conversation, but he doubted not its import. A heavy fall in stocks had shaken the market that morning, and the evening paper hinted that Hewson, the great stock-gambler, had, in the phrase of the street, "gone up." The next day would prove how the fall in the stock market had affected him.

Had the prediction of failure been with or without foundation? Farwell wondered, and watched the operator closely. He was a keen observer of character, and he had a reason for wishing to ascertain whether Hewson had lost or gained in the day's gambling.

The eager face of the financier wore its usual anxious expression. The lines about the nose were rather deeper than usual, and his hands fidgeted nervously with his bread. His appetite was not so good as it had been on the occasion when Farwell had last observed him, but the unusually hot day might account for that.

Farwell enjoyed his dinner. After the long period in which he had lived on the most ordinary diet, the well-cooked dishes of the *chef* were very agreeable. He was something of a Sybarite, and the few dainties prepared by his order would have tempted the most languid appetite. A certain pilaf served with boiled truffles, made from a receipt Farwell had obtained from a well-known gastronome, attracted the attention of Hewson from his own untasted dinner to the table of his neighbor. Farwell noted the look of interest in the tired face of the speculator, and without a moment's hesitation directed the waiter to present the

dish of pilaf to Mr. Hewson, with his com-
pliments.

It was a happy move; for the bored, worn
expression of Mr. Hewson's face changed to
one of pleasure, and the pilaf was fully appre-
ciated by him. He ate it with evident enjoyment, and with nothing of the mechanical
manner which often characterized him while
at table.

Farwell now knew what he wanted to.
The speculator was still a "financier," and
had not made a false throw. While success
attends the great operators they are given
the high-sounding title of "financier." An
unsuccessful attempt at "a corner," or a
"rush" in stocks which beggars them, wins
them the title of "gambler," long ago deserved, but only granted when the game is
up.

From Farwell's knowledge of the character and manner of Hewson, the appetite with
which he ate the pilaf and truffles convinced
him that whoever else had suffered from

that day's operations, Hewson had escaped
unscathed. Once convinced of this fact,
Farwell's next action was to leave the dining-
room quietly and hurriedly. His movement
did not escape the keen eyes of his neighbor,
and while he was lighting his cigarette in the
outer hall, Hangon the parasite followed him
and asked him to join Mr. Hewson over a
bottle of famous old Burgundy.

Farwell returned to the dining-room and
joined the two men over their wine. They
asked him about his journey with a certain
curiosity as to its end. Farwell gave them a
humorous account of his trip, with a graphic
picture of the life and manners in the town
he had lately visited. He was an excellent
talker at all times, and this evening he seemed
at his best; both men listened to him with
attention and interest.

Hewson, worn and wearied with the terrible ferment and worry of his life in the exciting atmosphere of Wall Street, was glad to
be taken out of himself and his own thoughts

by this bright and magnetic young man, whose slightly bronzed face and hands spoke of a long absence from the city. ˙ Hangon, tired with the long and close attendance upon the peevish patron, was thankful at so pleasant an addition to the *tête-à-tête* which had lasted for several days.

When Farwell finally rose to go, the two men followed his example, and the trio left the restaurant in company. Mr. Hewson's trap stood at the door awaiting him.

" Which way are you going, Farwell? Can I not give you a lift? "

The offer was made in a manner which showed that it was meant seriously, and not out of compliment.

" Thank you. I am bound on rather a wild-goose chase. I want to find Graball, and I have no idea whether he is at his house in Fifth Avenue or at Long Branch. Do you happen to know? "

" No. But get in and I will drive you up to his house; it is on my way. You will

look in this evening, Hangon, about eleven
o'clock?"

The mighty parasite nodded a reply, lifted
his hat, and with a sigh of relief at the two
hours of liberty granted him, walked off in
the opposite direction. Farwell and Hewson
drove up the long wide avenue past the
empty houses with closed blinds.

"How utterly desolate the city looks!
People are coming back later and later every
season." Farwell was the speaker.

"It's not wonderful," answered his companion in his peevish, fevered voice. "How
can any one be anxious, or even willing, to
come back to this cursed city a day before
they are obliged to?"

"How many days have you been out of
town this summer?"

"Every Sunday, and on the Fourth of
July."

"You have taken no vacation?"

"Not a day."

"How long is it since you have taken a
leave of absence from the city?"

"Not since I had the typhoid fever, three years ago."

"In all that time you have not missed a single business day in the street?"

"Not one."

For a few moments Farwell was silent. He was registering a vow that he would never allow himself to become so utterly demoralized, body and soul, by the demon of play, as was this poor nervous human being at his side. Hewson's millions at that moment numbered a score or more; his name was in the mouths of the whole army of gamblers, by whom he was envied, admired, and feared. It seemed to Charles Farwell that of all the unhappy human beings with whom he had been thrown in contact, Hewson, the great stock operator, was the most to be pitied.

Mr. Graball was not at home, the flunkey who answered the summons of the bell informed them. He had gone down to Long Branch, and would not be back that night.

Farwell was disappointed, or he appeared to be so.

" Will you take a turn on the Park ? " asked Mr. Hewson.

" Yes, thanks. Are you not afraid of malaria ? I am so much braced up by my long vacation that I should enjoy it, but is it wise for you to run the risk ? "

" Yes ; I am used to it. Do you think of returning to Colorado ? "

" Yes, it is possible. I have an interest in a claim there. It was apropos of that business that I wanted to see Graball."

" Is he interested in the scheme ? "

" No ; but I need the backing of Graball, or some such man, in the affair."

" Silver ? "

" Yes."

" Who owns the claim ? "

" A man named Cartwright, and myself."

" You want a company formed ? "

" In which I shall retain the controlling shares."

"Come round to my house and talk it over. If it is a good thing, perhaps I will take an interest in it."

This was what Farwell had hoped for. Of all the men he knew who could help him in the affairs of the Little Quickgain Mine, Hewson was the best to deal with, notwithstanding his crusty manner. Farwell's was a cautious, not over-sanguine nature, and he was sure of the value of the mine, and was moreover certain that he could convince Hewson of its value, once having roused his interest.

"Come to my rooms, if you will, Hewson. I have the papers and certificates of ore; you can look them over there."

He knew the advantage of being on his own ground, and preferred, in dealing with this man, to be the host rather than the guest.

CHAPTER XI.

" HALLO, Farwell! When did you get back, and how did you like Colorado? " The speaker was Mr. Gray Grosvenor; the place, the piazza of the Redwood Reading Room at Newport; the time, just half-past nine o'clock on a September evening. A cab had driven up to the door of this paradise of fashionable loafers, and Charles Farwell was paying the driver, when addressed by Mr. Gray Grosvenor.

" I am just from the boat," he answered, and joined his interlocutor on the piazza. " I liked Colorado immensely. What's going on in Newport? I have not heard a word from the place since I left it, nor seen a newspaper."

" You hurried back for the ball, I suppose? "

"Whose ball? I tell you, man, I'm just from the backwoods. I have not heard or thought of a ball for many a day."

"Oh," said Gray Grosvenor, and was silent. Strange chance that he, who was simply a club acquaintance, should be the first person to tell Charles Farwell of the ball given that evening by Mrs. Fallow-Deer on the announcement of the engagement of Miss Gladys Carleton to Mr. Cuthbert Larkington.

"Where did you say the ball was?" said Farwell, lighting a cigarette as he spoke.

Gray Grosvenor hesitated for an instant. Should he tell Farwell, who everybody knew had always been in love with his cousin, the news which he had evidently not heard? He had, somewhere about his stout person, the vestige of an organ which in his youth he had called a heart, and for an instant the promptings of that organ hindered him from speaking; but the thought of being able to tell people that he was the first one to break the news to Farwell came to him, and, as gossip was his profession, the chance of adding so choice a morsel to his store was too tempting to be lost, so he said slowly, his eyes fixed on Farwell's face, —

"Why, of course you have heard of the new engagement, — your cousin, Miss Carleton, to Larkington, that English fellow? Well, everybody knew it a week ago, on the day of the picnic, — ah, what a pity you missed the picnic! — but to-day it was officially announced."

He paused and looked at Farwell as if expecting a remark, and Farwell, having nothing else to say, only answered, " Oh, indeed!"

Gray Grosvenor was disappointed; he had a right to expect something more than the ejaculation of " Oh, indeed!" It would not sound very thrilling in the telling. But then Farwell's face was a thing to describe; it had grown quite white and set. " And so," he continued, " Mrs. Fallow-Deer is giving a ball to celebrate the joyful occasion. You'll go, of course? Everybody will be there, — quite the biggest affair of the season."

"No. I'm not invited, I fancy. I came back quite unexpectedly."

"But of course such an *intime* at the house as you are would not hesitate to go for the want of a card. Come along!"

"Thank you, Grosvenor, I have some letters to write." And, throwing away his unsmoked cigarette, Farwell walked into the quiet library at the back of the Club. It was empty, and, turning the gas low, Farwell threw himself into a chair, his back toward the door, and sat quite still for a space. His face was deadly white, under all the bronze he had acquired on the journey, and his forehead was lined with three deep furrows as he sat, his head leaning on his hand, deep in thought. When he moved at last, after a space of a quarter of an hour, his first action was a very strange one, and would have been considered by any of the men of the Club as extremely reprehensible, had it been seen. Fortunately it was not observed, for the room into which he walked was quite empty, save for a pair of sleeping figures in the two most comfortable armchairs.

It was the Reading Room, and on the tables lay piles of periodicals; among others, the New York afternoon papers, which had not yet been unfolded, and which a servant had that moment laid on the table. These papers Farwell quietly took, and, folding them into the smallest possible packet, put them in the pocket of his light overcoat, where was already a copy of the " Evening Telegram," which he had bought on the train, and read on board the Eolus, while crossing from Wickford, the terminus of the railroad, to Newport.

Leaving the Club, Farwell walked quickly along the avenue, and turned down the street which led to Mrs. Fallow-Deer's house on the cliffs. He entered the grounds, with which he was familiar, and walked to the back of the house, where he stood looking through an open casement at the brilliant interior.

The house was an excellent one for entertaining, though a trifle large and formal to be quite comfortable for every-day use. The spacious ballroom into which Farwell looked was oblong in shape, the walls were panelled in ebony half-way to the ceiling, and the furniture was of massive carved wood. " Veritable Antique" the old cabinet and *prie-dieu* were, but sadly out of place in this modern ballroom. The high throne-like chairs had in their day been used by cardinals and bishops, for they were from an old Episcopal Palace at Avignon, and the great clock had ticked away hours devoted to prayer in an Italian monastery. The sombreness of the dark wood was redeemed by the deep red color of the walls and the dull gold ceiling, the crystal chandeliers from Venice, the garlands of splendid roses, and the living flowers, tricked out in all that was most becoming and brilliant in toilettes and jewels.

At one end of the room stood Mrs. Fallow-Deer, resplendent in red satin and diamonds, her sturdy arms almost bowed down by the weight of the flowers with which she was burdened; at her side stood Gladys Carleton, dressed quite simply in a gown which Mrs. Craig rather spitefully characterized as " a white satin riding-habit."

It suited Gladys, who followed a fashion of her own in dress, and paid little attention to the " prevailing mode." She was as white as her dress, that night, and her eyes and hair seemed darker than ever, by the contrast of her pallor. On a stand at her side were heaped her bouquets, which, had she as many arms as the Hindoo idol, she could not have carried.

She was receiving with Mrs. Fallow-Deer, and many were the good wishes and gallant speeches made to her by the men and women of the world, who were on the whole very glad of the piece of good luck which had fallen to the beautiful Miss Carleton.

Gladys had all her life been petted and spoiled by her rich friends, and had never wanted for a good time, a fresh ball-dress, a seat at the opera, or a saddle-horse. She belonged to that class of young girls whose position in society is much better than their financial resources, and who for their beauty or their charm are the *enfants gâtées* of New York society. Instead of the spoiling which a rich father and mother can give, they enjoy the indulgence of a dozen foster mothers and fathers, who from the kindness of their hearts, or because they have no daughters of their own and know the attraction of a handsome girl in the drawing-room, socially adopt them, and stand sponsor to them from their first " season." For a very young girl it is a charming thing, but for a woman of Gladys Carleton's age and character it was a position not without its drawbacks, and her friends were all sincerely glad that she was about to be established in life so successfully.

Larkington, looking as flushed and radiantly happy as Gladys should have looked, stood near her, his eyes fixed intently on her face, his whole expression rapt and exalted. No one could doubt, in looking at the man, that he was deeply in love. The face, which had before lacked animation, and had been characterized by Mrs. Craig as "stolid," was now full of life and expression. All this was marked by Charles Farwell as he stood outside, his back turned to the slow-heaving ocean, and his feet crushing the roses of the garden that Gladys loved. He saw, too, the entrance of Gray Grosvenor, and the bow he made to Mrs. Fallow-Deer, watched him approach Gladys, and fancied he could almost hear him speak to her. He would tell her, of course — she started just then, and a flood of color crept up her white throat and spread over her cheeks and brow; yes, Gray Grosvenor had told her of his return. It

was the first unconscious movement she had
made since he had been watching her, —
that little start, and quick turn of the head.
She seemed to have grown restless, for in a
moment she laid her hand on Gray Grosvenor's arm, and disappeared with him out into
the square hall, where the crowd of butterflies was thickest, and there he lost sight of
her.

It was a brilliant spectacle at which Charles
Farwell stood looking, with the copy of the
" Evening Telegram " in his pocket, but when
Gladys left the room, its chief attraction
had departed. It was rather chilly in the
night air, and, drawing a cigar from his
pocket, he was about to strike a match, when
he perceived that he was not the only outside spectator of the scene; a man of low
stature approached him and stood looking
in at the window next the one where he had
taken his stand. Farwell did not care to be
seen, so he quietly put back his cigar in the
case, and the match in his pocket, and drew

back into the shadow cast by the angle of the bay window.

He could still see the interior of the ball-room, and, as he looked, he saw a servant approach Larkington and whisper something to him. The Englishman looked a little puzzled, bowed an assent, and after a moment or two, excused himself to the lady he was talking with, and left the room. The man at the window seemed interested in the movements of Larkington, and, as he left the ballroom, slipped quietly out of sight, disappearing around the corner.

A moment after he returned, and this time he was not alone. The tall figure of Larkington made that of his companion appear even smaller and more puny than before. They approached the spot where Farwell was standing, hidden by the dark shadow.

"Here," said the small man who, Farwell now saw, wore the livery of a groom, "stand here; on the other side of the house there's a crowd of people looking in at the doors and windows."

" Well, Stirrups," answered his companion, sharply, " why did you send for me in this way ? Could n't you wait till after the ball ? "

" No. I 'm just back. Jacob would n't let me have the money."

" D—— Jew ! Why not ? "

" Because, Cuthbert, you 've made a mistake somehow or other. It 's the wrong girl ; this one," nodding toward the ballroom, " is the cousin of the heiress, and has n't a penny to bless herself with."

" It 's a —— lie," cried Larkington, catching at the arm of his servant for support. " The Jew deceived you."

" It 's certain truth, Cuthbert, as I took pains to find out. It 's her cousin, an old maid, wot 's got the money, and no mistake about it. I made dead sure."

Larkington's only answer was a groan, and Stirrups continued, —

" We must be off on the early boat for Fall River ; it passes at two o'clock. I have packed the traps at the hotel, and will get the portmanteau down somehow by myself after the house is quiet. You must not return there, but must go straight to the wharf."

"Stirrups, I can't give her up," groaned Larkington. "Money or no money, I am crazy about her, and I will have her, if we go to the poorhouse afterwards."

"There will be another place than the poorhouse waiting you, Cuthbert, when those bills come in. Brace up, old man, the game is up. We have been in worse places and pulled through afore, only we have no time to lose."

"Stirrups, look here, I have made up my mind. I will marry Gladys, take her home to the old man, and confess the whole thing. When he sees her, he'll forgive me, and make it all right again."

"And who'll pay the parson and the travelling expenses? You're crazy, as you say. There's nigh a thousand dollars owing to these sharks of Newport tradespeople. And there's only ten dollars left, that I saved; just enough to take us out of this place to New York. Once there, I'll get a situation easy enough, and float us both till something turns up."

"I will borrow something from one of these fine friends of Miss Carleton. I have not borrowed a penny since I have been here. I won't run, Stirrups; that I swear. I'll marry Gladys Carleton if I blow my brains out the week after."

The two men had spoken in undertones, standing close together in the moonlight, but their voices had reached the ears of Charles Farwell, who disliked the rôle of eavesdropper and now stepped forward and joined the pair.

"If the excellent advice of your friend does not decide you to leave Newport, Mr. ——, I really am at loss for your name, — I think I have an argument which will prove more persuasive to you than any he has brought forward. Have the goodness to look over the telegrams from Egypt." And, drawing forth the copy of the New York evening paper, he put it into Larkington's hand.

At the sight of Farwell, at his first word, all Larkington's *blague* and assurance returned. " I do not understand you, sir," he answered coolly, and, stepping nearer the window so that the light from the ballroom might fall upon the paper, he read the paragraph to which Farwell pointed. It ran as follows : —

" ALEXANDRIA, Sept. —, 1882. In the engagement at Tel-El-Kebir to-day, there were twenty men killed, and an officer in the 60th Rifles wounded. — LATER. The officer who was seriously wounded to-day is Captain Cuthbert Larkington, son of Lord Lucre, of Oxfordshire, of the 60th Rifles. His recovery is doubtful."

CHAPTER XII.

GLADYS CARLETON woke early on the morning after the ball, which had been, everybody
said, the great success of the season. She
could not sleep, as she usually did after a
party, and after tossing for half an hour rest-
lessly on her bed, she rang the bell for her
maid, and stood looking out from the balcony
of her pretty room, as she had done that
morning on which she had promised to be
the wife of Cuthbert Larkington. It was
just such a morning as that had been, fresh,
clear, and full of sunshine. But it was of
another man than her *fiancé* that she was
thinking, — the man who had suddenly returned to Newport from Colorado, and whose
face she had not seen since she had become
engaged to the Englishman. Then she

thought, a little wonderingly, but quite in-
differently, as she had the night before, of
Larkington's abrupt disappearance from the
ball ; he had not even said good-night to her,
he had probably felt ill. The thought did
not seem to disturb her peace of mind, however, and she proceeded to make her toilet,
wondering the while what had brought Cid
back to Newport, — wondering and half guess-
ing. She hummed an old song, " We met,
't was in a crowd,"—and then sighed and
then laughed at herself for being sentimental.

The house bore the comfortless aspect
which always succeeds a ball, and, finding
the dining-room and parlors in the course of
being dusted and swept, Gladys stepped out
upon the green turf of the lawn, and walked
toward the rose-garden for a posy to put in
her belt.

"Who has been breaking the roses?" she
cried angrily, though there was no one there
to answer her question. One bush which
yesterday had been covered with splendid full

roses was broken, and the blossoms were trampled into the ground. She stooped to pick up one of the faded flowers, and saw a crumpled newspaper lying close at hand.

" How careless people are!" she ejaculated, and was just stooping down to pick up the paper when she heard wheels on the gravel driveway, and looking round saw Charles Farwell's trap coming up at a quick pace. He drew up the horses at the sight of her, and, giving his reins to the servant who had come out at the sound of the wheels, joined Gladys on the lawn.

" What brings you out and up at this hour, Gladys? it is not eight o'clock yet," were his first words, while he looked anxiously into her face.

" Why, I might ask the same question of you, Cid. How are you? I am so glad to see you."

" I forgot that I had not spoken to you before. Have you seen Mrs. Fallow-Deer this morning — or anybody else ? "

"You forget how early it is; no, I have not seen anybody. If you came to see Mrs. Fallow-Deer, you will have to wait; she may come down at ten." She was piqued at his queer, cool manner.

"No, I did not come to see Mrs. Fallow-Deer, or anybody but yourself. Come and take a drive with me."

"What? Before breakfast?"

"Yes; are you so hungry? We will drive to Finley's and get some grapes. It is a perfect day, and besides I want to see you, Gladys, for a few minutes. Come."

"I should like to — only I don't suppose I ought — I suppose you know, Cid —"

"Oh yes, I know all about what has happened in my absence. Run and get your hat, child, and take a drive with me."

"Well, I will, Cid." She plucked a rosebud from a bush which his careless feet had crushed the night before, and held it out to him, and then picked up the crumpled newspaper.

"What is that paper, Gladys? Have you been reading it?"

"No. I cannot imagine who could be careless enough to throw it on the lawn. Put it in the basket in the library, while I get my cloak."

Farwell gave a sigh of relief. He put the copy of the "Evening Telegram," which he had dropped the night before, in his pocket. She did not know yet, and he would be the first one to tell her the mortifying truth.

They drove down Bellevue Avenue, and out over Kay Street, stopping on the road to buy some rolls at a bakery, and some great bunches of black Hamburg grapes at a hot-house. Gladys laughed at her cousin, and said that she really could wait till breakfast time; but Cid broke off for her tempting little bunches of the fine grapes, and coaxed her to eat a roll. He had a great idea of fortifying the body before giving a shock to the mind. How pretty she looked that morning, all dewy and fresh as the wild flowers by the

road! The cheeks which had been so pale
the night before were rosy now, and the line
of her mouth had grown tender again. He
found himself looking at her and forgetting
all that had happened since the afternoon
when he had lifted her from her horse, and
she had given the little tired sigh, like a child
glad to be taken up by loving arms.

"Do you remember the last time we came
over this dear old West Road together, Cid?"
asked Gladys.

"Yes, it was the day before I started for
Leadville."

"Did you amuse yourself in Colorado,
Cid?"

"Well enough; but I did not go for
amusement. Here was the place where we
stopped and looked over at Fort Dumplings;
do you remember?"

"Yes, and I do believe there is the very
same man ploughing in the field."

Then they were silent, and the fleet horses
carried the light carriage at a flying pace

down the great hill at the two-mile corner.
The country was splendid with the glory of
the goldenrod, which lined the dusty road-
side and spread like a great yellow cloak
over the fields, cut into squares like a chess-
board by the crossing lines of the gray stone-
walls.   Some of the squares were deep green,
starred with purple asters; others were of
the rich brown color of new-ploughed earth;
many of the distant ones were yellow with
the harvested grain, and piles of deep red
gold pumpkins stood at the corners of the
fields.   The air was sweet with the smell of
the wild grapes which clung to the porches of
the bare unpainted farm-houses.   The beauty
of the complete and perfect year crowned
the fair earth, and the peace of the fruitful
harvest was over the land.   The air was
fresh, and, though full of light and warmth,
had a cool tinge in it, that set the blood running like new wine through the veins of the
man and woman who were so unreasonably
and unreasoningly happy, sitting, side by side,
behind the swift horses.

On they went, past the quaint old gray windmill on the left, whose four great white arms slowly revolved in the light breeze. In a little window high up in the quiet mill, which Gladys said looked like a giantess's thimble, they saw the miller's wife standing, a rosy child on her strong shoulder. The little creature waved its hand to the two in the carriage; he liked to see the horses and their shining harness.

"Why did you call me, Gladys, that day? A week ago yesterday afternoon, you called me, and I heard you in the depths of the earth, far, very far off; and now I have come to ask you why you called me, on the very day, they tell me, it was when you — when you had no right to think of any other man than the man you had chosen."

"I did not call your name; did you hear my voice?"

"I do not know if I heard anything with my ears, but your spirit called to mine and mine heard it; do you not know this to be true?"

"Yes, Cid."

"Well?"

She was silent, and looked away from his tender eyes, over the fair landscape, and then shivered at an ugly thought that came into her mind.

"Shall I tell you why you called me?" he asked. She did not speak, but bowed her head in assent. "Because you love me, Gladys, with a love which is not of this earth only; because your lower self tries to ignore this love, and would do it an outrage. Ah, child, you were in sore need of me when that spirit, so long subordinate to your worldly self, sighed to mine for help. I have come, and offer you that help." He paused, and then continued: "Why was it that at the last moment you threw over that 'splendid match' and gave such pain and mortification to that man in Germany?"

"I could not marry him, Cid."

"And why? Because you could not put a barrier between our two souls, which have felt the need so terribly one of another. We are free agents, Gladys, you and I; either of us by our acts could — can — break the union by which they are still bound. Would you bargain with your soul, child, for the sake of things which are of this world only, and wrong your spirit, by a bond of the flesh which would sever it from mine forever?"

The young man spoke earnestly and seriously, in a low voice, passionless and grave. It was not with such words that in the old days her boy lover had wooed her, and Gladys looked at him wondering, and yet understanding dimly all he said.

"If I should never see your face again, Gladys, you would love me always; do you not know it?"

"Yes, Cid."

They were silent again for a space, and Gladys noticed the drooping willows before the little gray farm-house, which with its wide pasture-land, filled with great sleepy cattle, seems the scene which Corot must have thought of in some of the strange pictures painted from a landscape seen only in a dream.

Gladys looked up into the eyes of the man at her side, which were turned half from her. There was no emotion in his face; he was quite still and silent, neither pale nor red, but with a far-away look of peace in his eyes, which shed a calm on her fevered, world-weary spirit. The quiet, still feeling which she saw on his face was nestling at her heart, and with the long, low sigh which shook her breast, all its weight of care and trouble, all the bitter littlenesses of her life, seemed to slip away from her, and in that moment of peace, full of a strange awe, the shadow of a love which should last for eternity swept over her soul.

A bird's note, calling to its mate, fell upon the quiet of the morning, and with the sound came the awakening. Farwell's eyes, which had been looking into the still blue of the skies, turned to seek those of the woman that he loved, who was so near him.

" Well, Gladys, shall it not be to-day ? "

She knew quite well what he meant, but, womanlike, evaded. " Why, what do you mean, Cid ? "

" You know well enough, dear. Shall it not be to-day that all the demons of pride and worldliness which have kept us so long apart shall be utterly routed ? Come, give me your hand like a brave girl, and tell me that you will be my wife before sundown."

" Cid, are you crazy ? "

" A little, perhaps; but how sweet a madness, is it not ? Better than the sanity which I have so long known. Come, give me your hand; that means yes ? "

" O Cid, how *can* you ? It 's wicked. Think of them all, — think of — that man."

" That is just what I won't think of. Gladys, I am in very deep earnest, much more so than you can guess. I ask you, dear, what may seem strange to you; but have you not all confidence in me ? I ask you to come now to Fall River, — why, we

are half-way there already,—and go to Cousin
Abel's house and ask the old fellow to marry
us. You know how gladly he would do it.
He made me promise, years ago, that he
should perform the ceremony which is to
make me the happiest man in the world. I
know all about the law. The license I can
get with his assistance in half an hour, and
little cousin Mary will stand as bridesmaid
to you in the parlor of the old house where
you first promised."

But to this hair-brained scheme the happy
girl would not listen, half because she loved to
hear him beseech her so earnestly, and partly
because, with her formal ideas, the whole
proceeding seemed well-nigh scandalous.

"What! no wedding dress or cake," she
cried,—" no reception, white slippers, or rice
thrown after us,—no one to give me away?
It would look as if I were afraid of my own
determination, and feared, if I did not marry
you right away, I should change my mind."

And the sorrels, brave creatures, still bore

the trap swiftly along, past Portsmouth, across
the middle road, and from the bold west side
of the island, over to the East Road, with its
wonderful panorama of river and islet, seen
from the high-road. Down Quaker Hill they
sped, through Newtown, and finally their
hoofs struck the timber of the Stone Bridge.

Gladys gave a little cry as she looked
down and saw the water beneath and behind
them. They had left the dreamy island,
" lying like an opal in a sea of sapphire."
Newport was behind them, and the wide
world before. At Tiverton they stopped,
and the horses were refreshed by a bucket of
cool water. To Gladys was no-need of water
or of bread ; Farwell never even thought
about his cigar.

Gladys still protested that she *would not*,
but she did not ask her lover to turn the
sorrels' heads towards Newport, and off they
started, the brave beasts, as fresh as if twelve
miles had not lain between them and their
stable. Gladys sang a little song, for the joy

in her heart could not speak in words; but as
the farm-houses were seen closer and closer
together, and the straggling outposts of the
town grew near, she became quite quiet, and,
slipping her hand into her lover's arm, looked
at him with eyes dark with a shadow half of
love, half of fear, — the sweetest look that
woman's eyes can wear, — the eyes of a bride.

" It was very strange that Gladys did not
come home to luncheon," Mrs. Fallow-Deer
said to Mrs. Craig, who had come round in
a state of wild excitement to tell the news
which the Egyptian telegram contained.

" So he was an impostor, after all," said
Mrs. Craig, after the two ladies had discussed
the matter for at least two hours, with the
assistance of Gray Grosvenor and Count
Clawski, who came to bring the latest news
about the strange affair, which was the talk
of the town.

Mrs. Fallow - Deer had been genuinely
shocked, and had wept real tears for Gladys's

disappointment and mortification, for which she felt herself in a measure responsible. She had brought down the letter of introduction which the *soi-disant* Larkington had brought her, and it was read by each and every one of the friends who had come to " talk it over." Now that she looked at it in this new light, the letter was a very guarded one, and the writer, an Englishman of more illustrious name than character, asked leave to present to Mrs. Fallow-Deer Mr. Cuthbert Larkington, whose acquaintance he had had the great pleasure of making on board the Servia.

Count Clawski, who had befriended the Englishman because he liked him, had brought the last news of him. Going down to the steamer to send off some important despatches, he had encountered Larkington on the gang-plank. The man had been too much overcome to speak, and had grasped the Count by the hand, and then staggered into the boat, accompanied by his servant

Stirrups, who had said, by way of explanation, —

"My master has had some bad news, sir,
which takes him away unexpectedly."

It was all very strange, — stranger that
Gladys did not come home; perhaps she
had seen the news in the morning paper,
and had gone to her cousin Amelia's house
to pass the day, and avoid meeting Mrs.
Fallow-Deer.

"Poor girl," cried that good lady at last,
when the final words had been said a hundred times on the exciting topic, and a hundred surmises made by Mr. Gray Grosvenor,
"I must really drive down to Amelia's and
find her."

It was three o'clock, the luncheon had
protracted itself until a very late hour, and
Mrs. Fallow-Deer, excusing herself from her
guests, rang for her carriage, and was just
preparing to start in quest of "the poor
deceived darling," when Charles Farwell's
card was brought up to her.

Into the great ballroom, which had lately
been the scene of Gladys's triumph, the good-
hearted matron went, trembling a little at
the interview before her with the only male
relative of Gladys who was likely to come
and ask her explanation of the unfortunate
affair.

There he stood by the mantelpiece, quite
composed and quiet, but with a face which
was bright with a light which had been missing from the ballroom on the night before.

On the sofa sat a queer little old gentleman with white hair and big spectacles,
whom Farwell introduced as "the Rev.
Abel Carleton, a cousin of Gladys's and of
mine."

Poor Mrs. Fallow-Deer! she had been
distressed at the idea of meeting one indig-
nant relative, and here were two. It was
almost more than she could bear, and, feeling that it was an occasion when a woman's
best card should be played, she pressed her
lace pocket-handkerchief to her eyes, and

sobbed forth a broken greeting to the two gentlemen.

"My dear madam," said the Rev. Abel, gallantly, "pray do not cry. It is my duty to break to you a piece of news."

"No, no, Mr. Carleton, I have already heard of it," wailed Mrs. Fallow-Deer, "and what *can* I say? No one can suffer more than I, at this sad affair; you certainly *must* know how entirely I was deceived by the young man."

"Indeed, ma'am, I was not aware that you had heard the news; but really, these tears, this distress — I cannot think, madam, that they are indicative of your real sentiments."

Mrs. Fallow-Deer bridled and dried her tears. "*Mr.* Carleton," she said in her most accentuated and dramatic manner, "I really do *not* understand you, sir; you seem inclined to make light of this terrible — this mortifying affair."

"Well, well, my dear madam, that is taking an extreme view of the case. It was without doubt sudden and perhaps rash; but, Mrs. Fallow-Deer, young folks are not so slow as we old ones in their thoughts or in their ways, and I thought sincerely that I was acting for the best in helping the young man —"

"What do you mean, Mr. Carleton? — Farwell, I don't understand it," said Mrs. Fallow-Deer, faintly.

"The fact is, dear Mrs. Fallow-Deer, I trust you won't be angry, but — Gladys —" stammered Farwell.

"Well, what about Gladys? Do you know where she is? I have not seen her to-day."

There was a little rustle, and from behind a curtain Gladys appeared, blushing, confused, radiant. She looked neither at Charles Farwell nor the Rev. Abel, but glided up to Mrs. Fallow-Deer, and, throwing her arms about that good lady's neck, buried her head on her tight-laced but motherly bosom, and whispered, —

"Dear, forgive us, — but I — am Charlie's wife."

L'ENVOI.

In the early October days Newport is still fair with a beauty tinged with sadness; the prime of the year is past. In the long crescent corridor of the Casino there is nothing of that gay throng of people we first saw there. Where hundreds were wont to sit and stare, walk and chat, only a dozen or two persons are to be seen scattered about. Among these few "late" people we recognize some faces on this October morning, whose acquaintance we first made in the merry month of August.

Mrs. Fallow-Deer, in the latest of Donovan's imported costumes, and Mrs. Craig, fresh as a rosebud, are sitting together, occupied for the moment in watching two people who are walking across the green that leads to the racket court. We can only see their backs, but that carriage of the head could belong to no one but Gladys Carleton — we beg her pardon — Farwell, and the light springing gait of the man at her side we have seen before, in the deeps of a Leadville mine. They had returned, the two young people, from their " trip," and the nine days' wonder of their marriage had been revived and seemed likely to live as many more days in the thoughts and conversation of the good people of Newport.

" Does not Gladys look handsomer than ever ? " said Mrs. Fallow-Deer, warmly.

" Oh yes, she looks very well ; but don't you think it's poor taste of them to come back to Newport, where they have been so much talked about, just now ? " said Mrs. Craig.

" Indeed, no, or I should n't have asked them to visit me. Why should they not ? I myself am proud of the girl who I always said had real heart, *au fond.* You knew that she never heard that Larkington was an impostor until a week after her marriage ? "

" I heard that Gladys *said* so," remarked Mrs. Craig, with a vicious intonation of doubt in her voice.

"I *know* that she did not know about it," rejoined Mrs. Fallow-Deer.

"Do you really believe that, dear Mrs. Fallow-Deer? Well, it is refreshing to find some one who is not sceptical in this day and generation. I suppose you believe also that Gladys did not know about Farwell's having made that pile of money in the Little Quick-gain Mine?"

"My dear, I *know* she did not, for when we talked it all over together that afternoon, after she came back, and surprised me into hysterics, she spoke quite seriously about her having married a poor man. She had always loved Charlie Farwell in a way, but she was a queer girl, and the knowledge of her love for him only came to her in its full force on that day when they went off for the fatal drive. She had loved him, but he had somehow failed to say the right thing to her; he had given her up too easily, before her heart was really awake."

"But," interrupted Mrs. Craig, "if she had

not heard all about that horrid Englishman,
she never would have done so queer, so
utterly unheard-of a thing as to get up in
the middle of the night and steal away to
Fall River, to be married by dear knows
who, to a man that she might have married
six years ago. It was because she had not
the face to stand the mortification alone, that
she took up with Charlie Farwell, who really
deserves better treatment."

"Now, Minnie Craig, once and for all I
won't hear any more such spite about Gladys.
It was because Charlie would not be taken
as a *pis aller*, that he married her that morning. He told her afterwards that if she had
not married him *then*, before she knew of
Larkington's being a humbug, and while she
thought Farwell to be a man of moderate
means, she never would have had another
chance. She never even knew there was
such a mine as the Little Quickgain, which
Charlie really only bought to help that queer
Bohemian friend of his, Cartwright, never

dreaming that his bread would come back to him toasted and buttered. Gladys married a poor New York broker, while she thought herself engaged to an English peer, just as surely as if the real Cuthbert Larkington had never been shot, and the false one discovered, and the Little Quickgain did not stand at 275. To her the credit of such unworldliness belongs, and only envy can deny it to her. It is not so often that we have a love match in our set; we had better make the most of it, I think."

The good Mrs. Fallow-Deer, at heart warm and kindly, spoke indignantly to the little pretty fribble of a worldling at her side, and Count Clawski noticed, as he joined the two ladies, that some rather high words must have passed between them, but he was too full of his subject to keep it to himself, he had a bit of news which he knew would be eagerly listened to by them both.

" I have just heard the real truth about our Englishman," he said, " in a letter from

my friend in London, to whom I telegraphed
to find out about him. His name is really
what he said it was, only he has not a right
to the Honorable, and he is not the son of
Lord Lucre. He is the son of a respectable
London retail haberdasher, of the same name
as Lord Lucre's family, Larkington, and, this
boy being born a short time after the son of
Lord Lucre, the mother thought it might
bring him good luck to give him the same
name as that of the Earl's son. His father
is a man of respectable position, but the silly
wife has had great notions of making a gentleman of her boy. She did not want him to
measure his betters for their socks, and so
raked and scraped together enough money
to keep him idle and floating about Europe,
as a gentleman of leisure. His groom was
his father's apprentice, and his great friend.
Lately there had been some row between
the father and son, and the two young men
started off for America."

Gray Grosvenor had joined the group

while Clawski gave this sketch of the bogus
Hon. Cuthbert, and after listening intently
to all the fat diplomate had to say, he heaved
a great sigh of relief.   No, Clawski had not
heard the *last* thing connected with the
strange affair, and his thunder was not stolen.
Rapturous thought!   As Gray Grosvenor
stood silent, a smile of superior knowledge
on his face, a warm complacency in his expression, awaiting the recovery of his breath,
lost in the quick pace at which he had walked
from the racket court to the corridor, his eyes
fell upon a picture framed in the oriel of
black wood in the balcony of the racket
court.   There, looking down at the group,
stood Gladys and her lover husband, smiling,
bright, and beautiful.   What a contrast they
were, — the Saxon-haired man, strong and
ruddy with health, and the graceful slender
woman with her white face and great dark
eyes!   For one moment they stood looking
down at their friends in the full sunlight, and
then Gladys waved a white hand, Farwell

lifted his hat, and they disappeared under the shadow of the balcony.

As they were lost to view, Gray Grosvenor gained his lost breath, and said, " Well, what do you think the last extraordinary act of that extraordinary young man is ? " Of course they could not guess and begged to be told.

" Why, the Farwells, passing through New York on their return from their queer bridal trip to Colorado, met Larkington in the street, looking seedy, sick, and generally broken up. Stirrups was with him, devoted still, but the two of them were in a bad plight. What does Farwell do, but pay the passage of these two rascals to Leadville, and give Cartwright directions to find them work in the mine, and let them have one more chance at supporting themselves honestly? What do you think of that ? "

Mrs. Craig sniffed and said, " It is not surprising that the Farwells wanted the man out of the way; he might talk and say some things which they would rather not have heard."

Mrs. Fallow-Deer said nothing, but pressed her handkerchief to her eyes, in which were real tears; she was rather hysterical that morning, and was easily touched.

"Ah! *noblesse oblige.*" Count Clawski was the speaker. For once the accomplished diplomate forgot his careful English and spoke feelingly in his native tongue. "*Vraiment, c'est agir en grand seigneur.*"

THE END.

University Press: John Wilson & Son, Cambridge.